PROLOGUE

DID LOVE DIE?

Angele had asked her mother that question once, after realizing her father, Cemal bin Ahmed al Jawhar—foster brother to the King of Jawhar and her own personal hero—was a serial adulterer. She'd been an extremely naive university freshman. So certain was she of her father's integrity, she had at first believed the tabloid story about him stuffed in her student mailbox was a hoax, a cruel joke played by someone who would never be called a friend again.

To this day, she did not know who had disliked her so much they'd felt the need to shred her illusions and with them, her heart.

Her first hero had tumbled from his pedestal and shattered at her feet, and he had not even known. Not to begin with.

Her still beautiful Brazilian former supermodel mother had looked at Angele in silence for several seconds. Eyes the same espresso-brown as her daughter's for once revealed her every emotion, and all of it staggering pain. "I would consider it a great blessing, but some of us are cursed to love unwisely and to do so until death."

"But why do you stay with him?"

"I do not. We live quite separate lives."

And another belief had been crushed under the pounding hammer of reality. They lived in the United States for the sake of Angele's education and the chance for her to be raised in relative anonymity. They'd made the modern country their home because Americans had plenty of their own scandal, they didn't have to go looking for it among the wealthy community from a small Middle Eastern country like Jawhar.

In a way, her mother *had* been protecting Angele. From the truth. But she'd also been protecting herself from the embarrassment of being the well-known wife of an undeniable philanderer. It had explained why their trips to Brazil and Jawhar were shorter and far less frequent than Angele had always wanted. It had also explained why her father's visits were equally brief, though far more frequent.

"Why not divorce him?"

"I love him."

"But he…"

"…is my husband." Lou-Belia had drawn herself to her full five feet eleven inches. "I will not shame my family, or his, with a divorce."

Considering the fact that Angele's father was considered a de facto member of the royal family of Jawhar, that argument carried some weight. Nevertheless, Angele had vowed never to be her mother that day. *She* would not be trapped in a marriage by duty and a helpless love that caused more grief than joy.

She had believed she was safe making the vow. After all, while no formal announcement had been made, Angele had been promised to Crown Sheikh Zahir bin Faruq al Zohra since she was thirteen years old. Heir to the throne of Zohra, no more honorable man existed in the Middle East, or anywhere else for that matter.

Or so she had believed. But that had been before today, when she'd received a packet of pictures of Zahir in the mail.

A sense of déjà vu washed over her, bringing back old feelings and memories so clear, she could still smell the spring grass clippings that had scented the air on that other fateful day a little over four years ago. The same cold chills washed up and down her spine, leaving a strange clammy flush in their wake.

If someone had asked her even one hour ago what one certainty she had, it would have been that Zahir would never be the center of a tabloid scandal. Besides being far too aware of his duty to his family and his position, Crown Sheikh Zahir simply had too much integrity to be caught in flagrante delicto with some woman.

Right. Her other hero.

Now, staring down at the topmost picture—an

FOR DUTY'S SAKE

FOR DUTY'S SAKE

BY

LUCY MONROE

First published in Great Britain 2011
by Mills & Boon, an imprint of Harlequin (UK) Limited.
Large Print edition 2011
Harlequin (UK) Limited, Eton House,
18-24 Paradise Road, Richmond, Surrey TW9 1SR

© Lucy Monroe 2011

ISBN: 978 0 263 22233 3

Printed and bound in Great Britain
by CPI Antony Rowe, Chippenham, Wiltshire

For Abigail and Jordan,
a very special niece and nephew-in-law.
I'm so proud of both of you, of all your
accomplishments and the love you two share.
May it bless you and may you live out your
own HEA with true joy and a fulfilment of the
dearest dreams of both your hearts.

almost innocent image of Zahir helping a busty blonde into the passenger side of his Mercedes, Angele choked out a strangled laugh. The barely there sound a pained constriction in her dry throat, the present took full hold with a snap.

Here, there was no smell of grass clippings, just the subtle scent of citrus her boss favored for the air ventilation system. No clatter of other students greeting one another in the common room of the University Center. Just the sound of her own breathing in the near-empty office.

The metallic taste of fear in her mouth mocked Angele and her hand shook as she pushed the topmost picture aside with her fingertip.

The next photo showed Zahir kissing the same busty blonde, though this time she was wearing a tiny bikini as they lounged beside a private pool. Angele did not recognize the couple's surroundings; the large Mediterranean-style house behind the pool could have been almost anywhere.

It was a popular architectural style for warmer climates, from Europe to South America.

She *did* recognize the passion between the two lip-locked people in the glossy eight-by-ten, though.

And it brought back a memory she would rather forget.

She'd been eighteen and in love with Zahir since she'd started having sexual feelings. She had not cared if others understood, or believed such a young girl was capable of the emotion. She'd known what she felt and it was not a simple crush, having grown deeper with each passing year.

She'd assumed Zahir had treated her with such restraint and kept his distance since the deal had been brokered because she was too young. But at eighteen she was formally an adult. At least by standards of the country she'd been raised in, the United States.

They were at a state dinner, their first time attending such an event as a couple. She'd thought it the perfect opportunity to share their first kiss and had brazenly cornered him in the courtyard.

Or as brazenly as a rather shy woman who had not been blessed with her mother's stellar beauty in the gene pool could be.

Filled with trepidation that could not stand against her determination, she had gazed up into eyes that had looked almost black in the dim light, though she knew they were gray. She'd grasped both his arms, her fingers curling around strong biceps that emanated heat even through his shirt and dinner jacket.

She'd tipped her head back, letting her own eyes close, and pleaded, "Kiss me."

Certain this man who was to be her husband one day would comply, *must* comply, she had waited in silent anticipation for what had felt like hours before gentle lips brushed her forehead.

Her eyes had flown open. "Zahir?"

"This is not the time, *ya habibti*." He had gently pushed her away. "You are still a child."

Crushed, she had been able to do nothing but nod and try to blink back tears of mortification.

He'd shaken his head and patted her arm. "Shh, *ya habibti,* our time is not yet."

As he'd escorted her back to the party, she had consoled herself with the implied promise and the fact he had called her his *darling.* Twice.

A harsh laugh barked out of her as the photo of him kissing that other woman blurred before her eyes. Angele was twenty-three and *still* waiting for him to realize she was no longer a child.

Without this photographic evidence, would she have ever realized that day was *never* likely to come?

Blinking away the moisture in her eyes, she focused on the pictures again, sliding one to the side and to reveal another beneath it until they were spread across her desk in undeniable evidence. This was not the first time she'd gone through the photos, but now she refused to look away, or stack them again neatly in an attempt to hide from what they represented.

Zahir did not think *this* woman was a child. No, Elsa Bosch was everything a man was looking for in a lover. Extravagantly beautiful, vo-luptuous, *experienced*.

Angele winced at her own assessment, know-ing she was none of those things.

She was not sure Zahir's honor was besmirched by his liaison with the German actress. Not yet. After all, *their* betrothal had never been formally announced and he'd treated Angele like a distant cousin, not a lover. Despite her clumsy attempt at eighteen to rectify the matter.

She'd allowed her own love and the future she'd believed they were meant to share to become the foundation for fantasies that shared no touch with reality. She'd believed that, one day, he would realize she was not the young girl the marriage contract had been negotiated around.

She'd been waiting ten years. *Ten years*. A decade in which she'd never dated, not even at-tending her high-school prom because she'd con-sidered herself taken. She'd had male friends in college, but none that she'd allowed to see her as anything but a study-buddy.

She'd just assumed that like her, Zahir had filled his life with family, responsibilities and friends…not a particular *woman friend*.

Unlike her own father, Zahir had been discreet in his relationship with Elsa Bosch. But the fact was: he'd had one.

These pictures could not be denied. So much like that time when she was at university, shouldn't her pain be every bit as profound?

But she felt hollow now. Empty. Devoid of the emotions that she'd nurtured in her heart toward him for so long.

Unlike that last time, this sender was demanding money in exchange for silence. If Angele did not pay, the note accompanying the pictures promised every American and European tabloid would get the opportunity to buy a set of photos along with a very embarrassing tell-all story.

The fact Zahir was having an ongoing affair with an actress who had starred in a skin flick was scandalous enough to cause considerable upset in the royal families of both Jawhar and

Zohra. Angele shuddered when she considered their response to a full-on exposé. The moment she'd gotten the pictures, she'd started researching the German actress.

While the woman spent less time in the spotlight than someone might expect, she was in no way a suitable companion for the heir to a kingdom.

However, Elsa was clearly his companion of choice.

These photos showed a great deal of skin, but even more passion. And happiness. *Zahir's happiness.* Angele had never seen him smile like he did in some of these shots. Even when he wasn't smiling, he had an air of relaxation he did not have around her.

Love might keep a woman married to a philanderer, but it might give another woman, a different type of woman, the courage to set the man she loved free.

Looking at those pictures, Angele knew deep in her heart that she could not allow Zahir to be held to a contract which had been brokered by men who had never given love between the two people involved even a fleeting thought.

Her love for him demanded more.

His lack of love for her demanded freedom.

CHAPTER ONE

HEART heavy with guilt at his envy, Zahir listened to his youngest brother speak his wedding vows.

Amir's voice came close to breaking as he promised, not just simple fidelity, but also love to his bride. Grace's eyes glistened, but her smile grew as she gazed at her groom with rapt fascination. Her own voice trembled as she returned the promise of love.

Love.

Both his brothers had found it with women not altogether suitable. But as neither were heir to the throne, their choices were hardly world-shattering. It was not the same for him.

His choice of bride had been set by an agreement between Zohra and Jawhar a decade past. His gaze skimmed the guests nearest the bridal party, gliding past his beaming father, king of their small Middle Eastern country, and his teary-eyed mother, to the woman he would one day wed. Though they shared no blood relation, Angele bin Cemal was treated as a favored niece by his uncle, the King of Jawhar.

Their eyes met, but she broke the gaze immediately, firmly fixing her gaze on the couple saying their vows.

He felt the dismissal, but was not surprised by it. Not after the past months preparing for the royal wedding.

Shocking everyone, the woman both royal families acknowledged would one day be *his* wife had refused to be a member of the bridal party or to participate in any meaningful way in the wedding. Citing her lack of close relationship to either the bride or the groom as her excuse, Angele had stood firm against every attempt by his mother and even Grace to include her.

Zahir had taken her uncustomary intransigence for what it was: a demand that he formalize an engagement between the two of them. Clearly she was done waiting patiently for her own nuptials. And, after the events of the past month, he realized the time had come to do his duty.

Besides, her father had kept his part of the bargain; he'd long since cleaned up his behavior so that he no longer courted tabloid attention.

After Zahir's mother had told him how devastated Angele was by her father's string of infidelities and the fact she had not spoken to the man in more than a year, Zahir had decided the time had come to do something about it. He wasn't close to his future bride, but Cemal would one day be a member of his family and Zahir wasn't about to stand by while the older man embarrassed *them* with his lack of discretion.

So, Zahir had laid down the law to Cemal. He'd told the older man that he would not marry a woman whose father's tabloid fame rivaled that of a European rock star.

Cemal had believed him. He'd patched things up with his wife and had not been featured in a scandal rag for almost five years, proving he took his daughter's future more seriously than his own marriage vows. Zahir kept the grimace such thoughts brought from his face.

He would never be that man—loveless marriage, or not.

He suspected that, unlike her mother, Angele would never tolerate it. Her surprising streak of stubbornness gave him hope for the years ahead. He did not want to tie his life to a doormat.

Regardless of how intriguing Zahir found this new side of Angele, his patience grew thinner by the minute as the wedding festivities marched forward. She took her stubbornness to a new, inexplicable level. She repeatedly declined to be in any of the formal wedding photos.

"Come, my little princess, I believe your point has been made." King Malik of Jawhar patted Angele's shoulder, his words showing he had put the same interpretation on her actions as Zahir had done. "Do not be the camel that tries to drink with its tail."

Angele smiled at her honorary uncle, though the expression did not reach her too serious eyes, and shook her head. "The formal shots are for family, not friends."

Stunned, and a little impressed, Zahir frowned. He had never heard her deny the king before.

"You are nearly family." *And would be soon enough,* Zahir implied, knowing she was intelligent enough to get his meaning.

She simply shook her head again and turned as if to go.

He reached out to grab her arm and then yanked his hand back, realizing what he'd almost done. They were not formally betrothed and to touch her so familiarly in this setting would be highly improper. As future king of Zohra, Zahir never acted without propriety.

At least in a public setting.

His behind-the-scenes impropriety was over as well, and he still felt a fool for pining after what he could not have.

A life of love and happiness, as his brothers

were building for themselves, was not to be for him.

King Malik laughed. "You begin to see the child as a woman with her own will, do you not?"

Zahir could not deny it. He had never seen Angele dressed with such an evident intent to entice, either. It had worked. He found her quite alluring. Used to barely noticing her at all, he'd been shocked by the low burn of arousal he'd felt when she had arrived. With new highlights shining in her dark brown hair, she wore it swept up to show off the slender column of her neck and the creamy, delicate slope of her shoulders.

The soft peach color of her couture dress was the only thing demure about it. Clinging to her slight curves, it fell inches short of her knees. While she did not share her mother's supermodel stature, in the dress and matching heels that added at least four inches to her height, Angele's legs looked every bit as long as the Brazilian beauty's today. And twice as sexy.

Add to that the fact that her stubborn refusal to participate in the wedding as a member-to-be of the family had intrigued him from her first refusal three months ago, and it was a lethal combination to his recently restrained libido.

Reminding him that his future wife had not been raised in the secluded environment inhabited by the women in the royal palace of Jawhar, she had continued to stand by her first denial. He'd been more than a little stunned to realize he liked it.

While his marriage would not be the love-match his brother had made, it would not be as much of a dry connection of two overly similar lives as he had always anticipated, either.

Frankly love could go hang, as far as he was concerned. This newfound passion and interest was all that he required, or wanted.

"Wasn't the wedding beautiful?"

A bittersweet smile curving her lips, Angela

looked up at her mother. "It was, but the love between Amir and Grace made it even more so."

"It reminds me of your father and my wedding." Lou-Belia sighed with a fond reminiscence that Angele found difficult to understand. "We were so much in love."

"I do not think Amir is like my father."

Lou-Belia frowned. "You know Cemal has settled down."

Angele did know. She still floundered in her feelings for a man who spent the better part of two decades flaunting his marriage vows, only to become the model of propriety in the face of his only child's betrayal-fueled rage and disapproval.

She was thrilled for her mother that the older couple's marriage seemed to be working again. The two spent a great deal more time together now, going so far as to live in the same domicile even. Her father was quite affectionate toward her mother these days, too.

But it hurt something deep inside Angele that

her father had not stopped his behavior until *she* had confronted him, and then refused to have anything to do with him for more than a year. What did that say of the strength of his love for his wife?

He'd pleaded with her mother to fix the breach between them and in the process, Cemal and Lou-Belia had found each other again.

"So, the past does not exist?" she asked helplessly.

"We let it go for the sake of the future." Lou-Belia's world-famous smile was soft but tinged with chiding. "It has been five years, *menina.*"

Little girl. Angele hadn't been her mother's little girl for a long time, no matter what Lou-Belia, or Zahir for that matter, believed.

Still, she gave her mother a tight hug. "You are a kind and forgiving woman. I love you."

But I don't want to be you, she thought to herself.

With that truth burning in her mind, she went looking for the man who would one day be king.

Some minutes later, Angele slid around the partially opened door to Zahir's office. He had disappeared from the wedding feast and she'd known she would find him here.

"Shirking your duty, Prince Zahir?" Her arms crossed over the sweetheart neckline of her short-short designer original. "Tsk, tsk, tsk. What would your father say?"

The room was very much like Zahir: masculine, rich and imposing. And yet there was something in the artwork and the old world furnishings that reflected more, something special—an appreciation for beauty that she knew few were aware of.

But while Zahir didn't pay her any particular attention, she had watched him closely and probably knew more about the real man than most. She still wondered at her ignorance of the secret revealed short months ago.

She'd decided it was willful blindness on her part, but that had not made her feel any better. Only mind-numbingly stupid.

She was a twenty-three-year-old virgin with no prospects and she knew she was to blame for that fact. She had clung to hopes and fairy tales that would never come true in the real world. Her parents' marriage should have made her realize that.

Zahir looked up from some papers on his desk, his gray eyes widening a fraction at the sight of her. He quickly stood to his full, impressive six feet four inches. He wore the traditional robes and head covering of a crown sheikh over a tailored suit that made him look mouthwateringly attractive to her.

Not that he was even remotely aware of the effect he had on her. She would have to be on his radar as an actual woman for that to happen.

"Princess Angele, what are you doing here?" He had always called her *Princess,* though she was not one.

But her godfather, King Malik, had nicknamed her such and the nickname had stuck. She'd always thought it sweet, but now realized it was one more barrier that Zahir kept between them.

His refusal to call her simply by her first name, as any man intent on marrying a woman might do.

He looked past her, no doubt expecting some kind of chaperone. But she'd left her mother and all other potential protectors of her virtue at the feast. She pressed the door closed, the snick of the catch mechanism engaging loud in the silent room.

"Have I forgotten we were to meet?" he asked, sounding perplexed, but not wary. "Did you expect me to escort you to the table?"

"I'm perfectly capable of walking to my own table." At her request, they had not been seated next to one other. "I know about Elsa Bosch."

She hadn't meant for that to be her opening salvo, but it would have to do. She'd paid the blackmailer, not once, but twice. After this weekend, Zahir's reputation would no longer be her concern. The picture taker would have to find another cash cow.

Distaste flicked over Zahir's features, at what she was not sure. Was he disgusted by the gossip rag that had printed a picture of him and his lover at a tête-à-tête in Paris the week before last?

Compared to the pictures Angele had seen, the two sitting at an intimate table for two was a boringly tame image. But as she'd suspected, the very fact Zahir was "friends" with the actress was cause for speculation and scandal.

Or was he disappointed in his prim and proper almost-fiancée bringing the subject up? She'd worked so hard for so many years to be the perfect image of his future queen.

Little did he know it, but *that* Angele was in ashes on the floor of her office back in America.

"That is not something you need concern yourself with."

Those words shocked her, hurting her when she thought no more wounds could be made. She had expected his anger. Disdain. Frustration, maybe. But not dismissal. She'd not expected him to believe that she had nothing to say about the women he shared himself with while leaving her untouched. Unclaimed. And achingly unfulfilled.

She wasn't ignorant. She knew that sex could and should be wonderful for a woman, but she was entirely inexperienced and she intended for that to change. Tonight.

The realization that Zahir had more in common with her father than she had ever believed almost derailed her determination but, in some strange way, it made it okay for her to make her bargain.

"The picture was rather flattering, to you both."

He stood up, "Listen, Princess—"

"My name is Angele."

"I am aware."

"I prefer you use it." If only for this one night, he would see her as a person in her own right. "I am not a princess."

And never would be now. Nor was she the starry-eyed child who had reacted with delirious joy upon the announcement of their future marriage. The past ten years had finally brought her not only adulthood, but a definitive check with reality.

The man she had loved for too long and if her mother was to be believed, would probably love until the day she died, had no more desire to marry her than he wanted to dance naked at the next royal ball. Perhaps even less.

"Angele," he said, as if making a great concession. "Ms. Bosch is not an issue between us."

He was so wrong. On so many levels, but her plan did not include enumerating them, so she didn't. "You were smiling in the picture. You looked happy."

Certainly he had never given Angele the affection filled gaze he'd given the German actress even in that single, oh so tame, picture in the tabloid.

Zahir looked at Angele as if she had spoken something other than one of the five languages he conversed in with extreme fluency.

"I read that you broke things off with her."
Angele had gone from supremely ignorant of
her fiancé's social activities to an expert on the
gossip surrounding him.

"I did."

"Because you were photographed together."

He frowned, but gave a quick jerk of his head
in acknowledgment. "Yes."

She found that sad. For Zahir. For herself. For
Elsa Bosch even. Had the woman realized she
was so expendable? Then again, she might well
have been the person who had extorted money
for silence from Angele.

Regardless, Elsa was not the real issue here.
And Angele needed to remember that, no matter
how hot her retinas burned with the images of
the other woman in Zahir's arms.

She pushed away from the wall and went to
look at the statuary displayed in a dark mahog-
any case. Her favorite was a Bedouin rider on a
horse, carved from dark wood. They looked like
they would race off into the desert.

But she noticed a new piece. It was another Bedouin, but this figure was only the man, in the traditional garb of the nomadic people. He looked off into the distance with an expression of longing on his features so profound her heart squeezed in her chest. "When did you get this?"

"It was a gift."

"From whom?"

He did not answer.

She turned to face him. "It was Elsa, wasn't it?"

His jaw locked and she knew he would not reply.

She refused to let that hurt her. "She knows you well."

"I will not lie. Our association was measured in years, not days." His tone had an edge to it that Angele had no hope of interpreting.

And his use of the past tense did nothing to assuage Angele's feelings.

"Yes, I gathered." The photos she had been sent spanned a timeline that could not have possibly been anything less. Someone who did not know and watch him so closely would not have noticed perhaps, but it had been obvious to Angele.

"The tabloids print trash. I'm surprised you read it."

She did not react to the taunt. Nor did she answer the implied question of where her information had come from. She said the one thing that needed saying. "You don't want to marry me."

"I will do my duty by my father's house." Which was more a confirmation of his lack of desire than she was sure he meant it to be.

"You'll make a great king one day." He was already an accomplished politician. "But that is not a direct answer and you neglected to note, I wasn't asking a question."

"If this is about Ms. Bosch and our now defunct association, please remember that you and I are not officially engaged."

"I am to take comfort in the inference you

would not be unfaithful if we were?" she asked carefully.

His brows drew together and for the first time since the discussion started, she saw anger make its way to the forefront. "Naturally."

"I don't."

"Don't be ridiculous, Prin—Angele, I am not your father."

"No, you aren't." And she would never give him the opportunity to prove them both wrong, either. "This isn't about Elsa Bosch, not really."

Ultimately it was about love. It was about loving someone enough to let them go. Only that sounded so cheesy, she'd never speak the words aloud. And it was about knowing she deserved to be loved, fully and completely, by the man she would spend the rest of her life with.

He did not look like he believed her claim and she could practically see the thoughts zinging around in his facile brain. He was trying to figure out the right words to reassure, when in fact none existed.

None that he could say anyway.

Again it was time for truth. "Your brothers have both found wonderful happiness while you have been stuck in a promise made on your behalf by two men with too much power and too little comprehension of the cost of their dynastic plans."

"I do not consider myself stuck. I was an adult when that agreement was made." Yes, he'd been all of twenty-four and as bound by duty as any young adult male could be. "I chose my future."

An alpha male like Zahir would have to convince himself of that, or he could not accept the limitations imposed on him by others. It simply was not in his nature. He had the heart of a Bedouin, if also the responsibilities of a landed royal.

"You do not wish to marry me," she repeated, refusing to be sidetracked. "And I won't let you be forced into doing so by duty."

Nor would she allow herself to be railroaded into a marriage with the potential to be every bit as miserable as her parents were for so many years.

His eyes narrowed, his expression turning even more grim than usual. "You are not making any sense."

"We've been promised for ten years, Zahir. If you had wanted to marry me, we would already be living in wedded harmony here in your family's palace." They would definitely at least be formally engaged.

"It has not been the right time."

She'd heard that argument before. And believed it. First, she'd been too young. Then, his father's health had been precarious. The idea of announcing an engagement during such a time was not appropriate, or so Zahir had claimed. Then, Khalil had gotten engaged and stealing his spotlight during the preparations for, celebration of and immediate time after Khalil and Jade's wedding would have been wrong. The same excuse came convenient to hand when Amir and Grace became engaged.

For ten years, five—if you only counted the years since she became an adult—they had not found the right time to announce their engagement, much less actually get married. And they never would, if it meant finding a time when Zahir *wanted* the nuptials to take place.

Though Crown Sheikh Zahir bin Faruq al Zohra would no doubt eventually allow duty to force him into following through on a marriage he did not desire.

Since she would be the other half of that marriage, she wasn't going to let it happen. Realizing that had meant giving up her dreams. And that had hurt, even more than seeing the photos of Zahir kissing Elsa.

But then who was Angele kidding? Certainly not herself. Seeing the unfamiliar happiness on Zahir's face had lacerated her heart far more than the passion. The numbness having long since given way to a devastation she would have happily avoided for the rest of her life. And her heart was still bleeding.

Better that, than a lifetime of pricks from the knife edge of the constant knowledge that she was not the woman her husband wanted to be with however. When she'd conceived her current plan, a steel band had formed around her chest, and that constriction was still there. Sometimes, she felt like it was the only thing stopping her from falling apart.

But that, too, would fade. Eventually. It had to.

How much worse would it be to live the rest of her life married to a man who did not love her and never would? Who did not even like her enough to spend any time with her not dictated by their roles and responsibilities?

To watch Zahir find joy in the arms of other women as her father had done over and over again? Angele wasn't about to go that route.

Even after receiving the packet of pictures, funnily enough it had been the announcement of Amir's marriage that had settled the issue for her. Amir had been meant to marry another member of a powerful sheikh's family, but Lina had refused the match and Amir had ended up married today to the woman who held his heart instead.

As Angele had told her mother, Amir and Grace's very real love had made the wedding ceremony beautiful.

What she had not told her mother was that she had seen the envy in Zahir's expression when he had looked at Amir as he stood up with him. No one else had noticed, of course, but Angele had spent a lifetime watching Zahir with more attention than research scientists gave their life's work.

Lina's courage had given Angele the courage to come up with her plan. And Amir's happiness today had cemented her determination to follow through with it. If there was any chance Zahir could know his brother's happiness, he deserved to have it.

She could do no less for the man she loved with her whole heart.

And she would accept nothing less than that,

either, even if it meant spending the rest of her life alone.

"Zahir, I have always found you to be honest. A man of deep integrity." His liaison with Elsa had not changed that.

As he'd pointed out, Angele and Zahir were not actually engaged. And he had never once lied about it. She'd simply never thought to ask point-blank if he had sex with other women. However, she was no longer rock-solid in her belief he would not take mistresses after their marriage. In fact, that certainty had died a pretty painful death.

No matter what he'd said today.

"I am."

"Are you in love with me?" One of those point-blank questions she could not avoid asking. Not now.

He did not even blink, his handsome features set in an emotionless mask. "Our association is not a matter of love."

"No, I know it isn't, but please, this once, just answer my question with a simple yes or no."

His jaw tightened.

"Please."

"I do not see why you would ask."

"I'm not asking you to understand, simply to answer."

"No."

She almost asked if his negative was a refusal to answer, but then she looked into his gray eyes and saw the smallest glimmer of pity. He knew she had feelings for him he did not return.

The pain his answer caused wasn't mitigated by the fact she'd been expecting it. Though she really wished it had worked like that. Knowing he did not love her and hearing it from his lips were apparently in totally different realms of experience.

She managed to nod. "That is what I thought."

"Love is not necessary in a marriage such as ours."

"I don't agree. I will not marry a man who has no hope of loving me."

"I—"

"Have not found something worthy of love in my person in ten years—you are not likely to find it now." In fact, she was so certain of that impossibility, she was ready to take desperate action.

"You are all that is admirable in a future princess and eventual queen."

But not as a woman he could love. She left the words unsaid as he did. "You deserve the happiness your brothers have found."

"It is not in my stars." His tacit agreement sent another javelin of pain straight through her, but she refused to buckle under the fresh wound.

She had a plan and in the end, it would be best for both of them. "It can be."

"I will not turn my back on my duty." And his tone censured her for suggesting he try.

"I will."

CHAPTER TWO

ZAHIR felt those two small words like they were blows from the strongest of sparring partners. Part of him had always expected some kind of betrayal from Elsa Bosch, though not to the extent she had gone to. He had never been able to give her what she craved: commitment for the future.

However, he had believed Angele a woman of supreme honor and understanding of her duty.

"You are not serious." He looked closely, trying to see evidence of too much champagne, but her pupils were not dilated.

Her cheeks were flushed, but the topic of their conversation could easily account for that.

"I am." She looked down at the Bedouin figure and reached out to touch it almost wistfully. "I will not allow you to be locked into a marriage with a woman you cannot love."

"And you expect to be loved by your husband." Where had she gotten her romantic notions of marriage? Certainly not from her parents.

"Yes."

"You appear to forget the importance of duty and family obligation."

A deep, burning anger flickered briefly in Angele's dark eyes. "My mother's adherence to duty is one of the primary reasons I am so determined not to follow through on this farce of a marriage."

"There is no farce in joining the royal houses of Zohra and Jawhar."

"I am not of the royal house of Jawhar, no matter how indulgent King Malik is toward me and my father."

It was true. From one of the most influential families in Jawhar, Cemal had been fostered in the royal household when his parents died. He'd been raised like a brother to Malik, but they shared no blood relation. Which had actually played in favor to the agreement drawn up ten years before as Zahir and Angele had no blood common between them.

"I did not think this bothered you."

"It doesn't."

"You cite it as reason for not keeping your commitment."

"I never made a commitment. When I was thirteen I was informed that one day we would marry."

A mere girl. He had felt compassion for her. "But you never complained. Why now?"

"I spun fairy castles in the air, dreams that took me too long to realize they had no basis in reality."

Dreams of love. Didn't she know? That commodity was not for such as them. "You need to consider this more carefully."

"Zahir, I'm giving you your freedom." Exasperation and a tinge of anger laced her tone.

"Instead of trying to talk me out of it, you could simply say thank you."

Did she really believe she was doing him a favor? He did not think so. "Our families will be shamed."

"Oh, please. Nothing official has ever been announced."

"Nevertheless, the expectation exists."

"So?" She shrugged, as if really, this did not matter. "Those who have expectations will have to be disappointed."

"Like my father. Like the man you call uncle. They will be humiliated."

The look she gave Zahir said she did not buy his calamity scenario. "Disappointed maybe but, in that regard, not as much as they would be by a divorce."

"Why divorce?" Though he admitted he did not know her as well as he could, he had never considered her a pessimist. "You are not making any sense."

"Zahir, can you honestly tell me that you are

not feeling even a little niggle of hope right now? That relief isn't warring with your need to talk me out of doing what you know you want?"

Shock held him silent. Her words implied that she actually believed she was doing him some sort of favor; that somehow he would and even *should* thank her for threatening to break her word. He tried to think of what could have caused her to draw such a ridiculous conclusion, but despite his superior intellect he came up with nothing.

No possible reason for her outlandish ideas.

She sighed, her shoulders slumping just enough that he knew she was not as calm about this as she was pretending to be. "Your silence speaks better than your words could. I will take full responsibility for the aborted engagement with our families and the media."

"No." He surged up from his desk, realizing that perhaps now was not the time to intimidate with that barrier between them.

"I have only one request."

He halted on his way around the desk. "What is it?"

"I want one night in your bed, the wedding night I will not now have."

If she had shocked him with her threat to break their agreement, this request practically had him catatonic. What in blue blazes was she *thinking*?

"Why?" he ground out while trying to somehow make sense of his prim and proper princess-to-be offering him, no, *demanding* from him, something that should not be indulged in until after their marriage.

The next heir could not be conceived under a cloud.

"I want you to be my first."

Well, naturally. "But you do not wish to marry me."

Did she truly believe there was any sense, even the smallest modicum of logic in such a scenario?

"Did you want to marry Elsa Bosch?"

He'd indulged in fantasies at one time. He'd believed himself in love. More fool him. But even then he'd known it was pure fantasy to even consider such a thing. He'd soon realized that more than her career made her the wrong choice as future queen of Zohra.

Even in his most youthful exuberance of untried emotion, he had not been a fool. "It was not a consideration."

"But you had sex with her." The blunt words falling from Angele's usually prim mouth added to his sense of falling down the rabbit hole.

It was time to put a stop to this conversation. "That is not something I will discuss with you."

"I'm not asking you to—I'm simply making an observation."

"This entire conversation is insane."

"No, what *is* insane is two people prepared to marry for the sake of nothing but family obligation in the twenty-first century."

Her American upbringing had much to answer for.

"I will one day be king. The woman who rules

Zohra by my side must be a suitable match." Angele knew this. He should not have to repeat it for her. "*Love* has nothing to do with the obligations you and I must uphold."

"You say it like it's a dirty word."

It was his turn to shrug. In his life? That particular emotion had caused more pain than pleasure.

"Your brothers have both found love."

"They do not have the responsibilities of the crown to uphold." And neither man had had a particularly smooth road to *true love*, either.

Zahir had no desire to follow in their footsteps in that regard. He had enough of his own challenges in life to face as ultimate leader and servant to his people.

"Your father doesn't wear a crown."

"Don't play semantics with me—this is too important." He could not believe she was saying these things. "I believed you understood the importance of your obligations."

"My greatest obligation is to myself. I know

you don't see it that way." She quoted an Arabic proverb he often used that was strangely apt to their situation. "I'm not that person. I don't believe countries will topple if their leaders seek personal happiness in a manner of integrity."

"What is honorable about breaking our engagement?"

"We aren't engaged."

"As good as."

"Really? You truly believe that?" she asked as if his answer carried great import.

"Yes."

Unutterable sadness came over her features and the light in her eyes dimmed. "I'm sorry."

"You will give up this idea of backing away from our wedding?"

"No." Her voice was laced with determination, but there was a flicker of fear in her expression.

And suddenly, he thought he understood. Things that made no sense began to fall into a picture he could comprehend. *She was concerned about their compatibility in the bedroom. As well she might be.*

In one respect, she was spot-on. They were not a nineteenth-century couple where the bride and groom had been expected to go to the marriage bed untouched. Or, at the very least, the bride.

She'd spent her life in the United States, surrounded by a culture that had demystified sex and frequently glorified it. He had never made improper advances because, despite his claim, they were not actually engaged.

At first, Angele had been too young, and later he'd had his liaison with Elsa. A relationship doomed from the beginning, but one that allowed him to come as close to escaping the stranglehold of his everyday responsibilities as he ever would, if only for the brief moments they'd had together.

He had foolishly allowed his emotions to get involved. So, when he'd discovered he was not her only lover, he had been hurt. And he was still angry with himself for being that vulnerable.

In the midst of his own self-allowed turmoil

and the growing crush of his responsibilities without outlet, he had neglected to notice the impatient discontent in the woman he was slated to marry. Yet another casualty to the folly of allowing emotions to reign in one's life.

Angele shook her head and glared at him. "Stop it."

"Stop what exactly?"

"Thinking so hard. I just know you're trying to figure out a way to guilt me into maintaining the status quo. And that is not going to happen."

"No, I can see it is not." Angele needed reassurance that their marriage would not be devoid of passion.

Something he had done nothing to convince her of in the intervening years since the original contract was negotiated. Considering how his member stirred in his trousers at the sight of her in the sexy dress, he knew he would have no problem reassuring her now, however.

"You want to have sex with me."

She flinched, but squared her shoulders and

nodded. "I'm offering you your freedom. I do not think a single night of lovemaking too high a price to pay for that."

The words were just noise to cover her sexual fears and insecurities. He understood that, but one thing stood clear. She considered a night in his bed a gift.

He looked deep into her eyes and made another realization—one that both inexplicably pleased him and stirred pity in his heart. "You are in love with me."

Zahir had always known Angele fancied him something rotten, but he'd considered it a mere girlish crush. However this woman before him was no child and the feelings so apparent on her features had a depth that shocked him. Love was not a comfortable or safe emotion. From this point forward, it would not hurt her to love him, but she did not know that. He would never betray her as Elsa had betrayed him.

"What was your first clue? My clumsy attempt at a kiss at eighteen, or my slavish devotion and refusal to date other men despite the fact we are not formally engaged?"

If he expected shock from her at his revelation, or horror, he would clearly receive neither.

He did not point out that her love for him made no sense in light of her demands and threats to back out of their families' arrangements. He had already decided she had no real desire to do that, she was simply looking for reassurances.

The need for which made even more sense in the light of her feelings for him.

Nor did he point out that her love was based on a distant relationship. How could she know him well enough to love him? But she believed herself in love and that was enough to cause her pain and worry in their current situation.

"I apologize for not realizing your feelings sooner." Acknowledging the hurt she must have experienced over the years of their pseudo-engagement, was not comfortable, but he was not a man to shirk from his responsibilities. "Love is a painful emotion."

"You're telling me?" she asked with disbelief and then the horror came. The color drained from her face as her eyes registered a mortal wound. "You *are telling me…*that you loved her."

For the first time in his life, he was tempted to outright lie. He had learned the art of misdirection and when it was most politic to withhold information at an early age, but he made it a practice never to tell a direct falsehood. Even for the sake of politics.

His honor would not stand for it.

"It does not matter. Ms. Bosch and I are finished."

"But you loved her, didn't you?"

"That is not something I'm ever going to discuss with you." The past was over. He and Angele had a future to build.

His youthful feelings embarrassed him and they were over regardless.

"You don't need to. The photos show the truth, if you look for it. I didn't…I don't think I wanted to believe it was possible. It was painful enough to accept you were so much more relaxed and happy with her."

"You gleaned all this from a single photo?"

"No, but that's not something *I* want to discuss right now."

No, right now, she wanted reassurances he was more than happy to give. Nevertheless… "We can hardly disappear from my brother's wedding feast."

"Why not? You did."

"I had business to attend to if my father was to remain free to preside over the festivities."

"You often sacrifice for your family."

"It is my privilege to do so."

"I believe you mean that."

"I do."

"You're an amazing man."

"And you love me." He had no intention of opening himself to that depth of emotion again, but he would protect hers. It was his duty to do so.

And he always did his duty.

"The wedding festivities will last into the wee hours of the morning. Tonight is not the ideal time for us to share our bodies for the first time."

"What do you suggest?"

"You are in the country for the next three days?"

"Yes, we're staying for the full wedding celebration."

Despite Angele's refusal to play a role in the wedding, her family had been at the palace since the prewedding festivities began. He had seen very little of her because he had been busy with state business. He had believed she was busy with the bridal party, even if she wasn't an official member of it.

"I will make arrangements for your last night here. There are no official events after the final breakfast that day."

He put his arm out. "Now, I believe it is time we returned to the feast."

She laid her small hand in the crook of his arm and let him lead her from his study, the stress this discussion had caused her evident in the fine tremors of her delicate fingers against his jacket sleeve.

Two nights hence, he would show her she had nothing to fear from him in any way.

Despite the sun having set an hour before, the tile floor on the balcony off Angele's room warmed her bare feet. She'd long since discarded the expensive but uncomfortable glittery heels she'd worn for the final celebratory feast of Amir and Grace's nuptials.

She still wore the figure hugging silk sheath. By an as yet undiscovered New York designer, its subtle composition made the most of her figure, hinting at bedroom seductions while having no single element that could be pointed to as anything other than proper.

Her father had been angry she'd foregone the traditional dress the women of the Jawharian royal family had opted to don for the evening feast. Only Angele *wasn't* a Jawharian princess, no matter how much her father might wish otherwise.

Her mother had stood up for her. Looking like American royalty in a beautiful European-designed gown, Lou-Belia had told Cemal to take a chill pill. The look on Angele's father's face had been worth the price of admission and then some.

But the expression that flashed over Zahir's features when he'd seen Angele's dress had been even better. His gray eyes had heated to molten metal and his lids had dropped in a look of pure sexual predatory interest before he'd schooled his features into diplomatic blankness. It hadn't been just the once, either.

She'd caught that heated stare directed her way more than once over the course of the evening. Each time, it increased her desire for the feast to be over, for her one night with Crown Sheikh Zahir bin Faruq al Zohra to begin.

The celebration *was* over now and she could go to Zahir as soon as she wanted. The only thing stopping her was the garment lying so innocently on her bed.

She'd discovered the *galabeya* upon returning to her room. The traditional wedding dress in this part of the world, the white silk gown embroidered with gold thread looked like it belonged in an *Arabian Nights* fantasy. The Arabic lettering in the intricate embroidery told the story of the first Sheikh's marriage to the wife that helped him found the house of Zohra.

A note from Zahir lay atop the *galabya*.

My dear Angele,
You indicated a wish to have a wedding night. Please do me the honor of wearing this gown, worn by my grandmother in her wedding to my grandfather.

I look forward to seeing you in and out of it.

Zahir

The day before, he had told her to come to him via the secret passages she'd never known for certain existed. She'd guessed, since the palaces in Jawhar all had them, but Angele had never been privileged with that information regarding the royal palace of Zohra. Until now.

Now, when she planned to leave the palace of Zohra tomorrow and never return to it.

With a deep sigh, she turned from the darkness toward the warm light emanating from her bedroom. The *galabeya* shimmered under the glow, calling to and repelling her with equal fascination.

He wanted her to wear a wedding dress on their single night together. It was mind-boggling, but not nearly as shocking as it should have been. Part of her wanted the fantasy. Her subconscious at least was on the same page as her soon to be former almost-fiancé.

So, why balk at his request? The *galabeya* was easily the most beautiful one she had ever seen, the needlework making the Arabic letters look like art and perfect in each stitch. The matching slippers were beyond elegant. And looking at them, she knew they were exactly her size.

How had Zahir managed that?

A tiny voice warned against the cost tomorrow to that kind of indulgence tonight. But it was her *one night,* the only time for her to be with the man of her dreams. Perhaps it would make the morrow harder, but she would not balk at letting it fulfill every fantasy possible.

She changed into the *galabeya,* shivering with a sensuality she'd kept locked deep inside since her first sexual feeling, as the silk whispered against her skin. She'd opted to wear a modern bra and panties in matching white silk and lace, rather than the traditional underclothes Zahir had left with the dress. After all, this wasn't a wedding, but a seduction.

Though she was not at all sure any longer who was seducing whom. Certainly Zahir showed none of the reticence about bedding her that he always had done before.

Perhaps it was because his relationship with Elsa had ended. The one and only time their picture together had featured in the media, it had quickly been followed by a discreet announcement that any liaison there might have been between the two had ended.

In addition, Angele could not let herself forget the offered price for this night was ultimately Zahir's freedom. Perhaps that, if not she directly, accounted for his increased ardor in her regard. Whether or not he was willing to admit it, he clearly wanted out of their pseudoengagement.

Or had he always been attracted to her in some fashion, but unwilling to act on it because to do so would force the issue of their marriage?

She preferred that scenario to the one where he found the prospect of freedom so appealing, it alone birthed lust in him over her body.

Refusing to analyze the confusing situation any further, she brushed out her hair and changed her makeup to a neutral palette with eyes that were rimmed in kohl.

If not for the highlights in her hair and barely there underclothes, she could have been a bride of Zohra from a hundred years ago. She saw no one in the secret passageways, but heard a peal of feminine laughter as she passed the access to what must have been Amir's rooms.

It sounded much too close to be muffled by walls. Having no desire to be caught on her way to Zahir's room, Angele scooted into a crevice as the sound of bare feet padded down the passage she had just passed.

"Shh…the operative word here is secret," Amir said in a loud whisper to his still giggling wife.

"How did I not know they existed all the times I stayed in this palace?"

"You were not yet my wife."

"I am now." Grace sounded both awed and very pleased by that fact.

"Indeed." Amir's voice was laced with pure possession, however.

"So, are we going to explore?"

"Would you rather do that, or return to our rooms and celebrate our marriage?"

"Guess." Silence filled only with the sound of kissing and increasingly heavy breathing followed. Then, Grace said in a husky voice, "This week-long wedding thing is pretty neat, I must say. Western brides only get one wedding night."

Their voices faded as the footsteps returned the way they had come and Angele released a pent-up breath. She did not know how Zahir had stood maintaining a hidden affair for so long.

One night was enough to stretch Angele's nerves tighter than a model's corset….

CHAPTER THREE

SHE made it to Zahir's room without further incident. Then she stood in front of the lever that would swing an ancient wardrobe within the room open like a door, and gathered her courage. This was it. The moment she'd craved far longer than anyone else would ever know.

She reached out to pull the lever, but the "door" was already opening. It swung inward to a room lit by numerous candles.

Clad in the traditional wedding garments of the Zohra royal family, Zahir looked at her with an expression so serious, it made her breath catch. "I began to think you had changed your mind."

Unable to speak, she shook her head.

"Your wedding night awaits." He stepped back. "Come."

Her heart hammering, she followed him into

the candlelit room, but jerked when he reached behind her, and then blushed at her jumpiness.

"Be at peace. I am only closing the access to the corridor."

"Can just anyone come in through it?" she asked, another worry finding its place in her maelstrom of emotions.

"Only the family knows of its existence, and a select few of our security detail, those whose families have served the royal house for generations."

"But still." What if his brother, or father, or something, decided to make a late night visit?

"I have locked it from this side. The lever on the other side of the wall will not move."

Relief washed over her. "Amir and Grace were in the corridor."

Zahir's entire body tensed. "Did they see you?"

"No."

He nodded, relaxing a little. "It would not have been a total tragedy, but I would prefer you not to be made the object of speculation."

She begged to differ. If she'd been seen, dressed as she was, it *would* have been both humiliating and a huge and total tragedy. Nothing would stop her uncle from forcing the marriage if she were caught in such a circumstance.

Thank goodness, only the royal family of Zohra knew of the passages. And her.

"How did you know I was in the corridor? Is there some kind of alarm?"

Zahir merely shrugged, but there was an odd expression in his eyes, the soft light of the candles giving his angular cheeks a burnished glow that almost looked like a blush.

He reached out and cupped her cheek. "You look beautiful."

"You didn't like my dress earlier?"

"You know I did."

"Do I?"

"Oh, yes." His hand slipped around her head and settled against her nape. He used the hold to gently tug her forward until their bodies were a mere breath apart. "You are a minx. How did I not realize this before?"

"Minx is such an old-fashioned word."

"I am an old-fashioned guy."

"You think?"

"In some ways, I am very traditional."

Then, before she could answer, he lowered his head and she finally got the kiss she'd always wanted.

And it was every bit as tender and romantic as she could ever have hoped. Letting out a little sigh of pleasure, she let her lips part slightly.

Zahir's tongue swept inside, claiming her mouth with unhesitating, if gentle, demand. Her arms moved of their own volition, her hands clasping behind his neck as she melted into him. His big body shuddered at the full-on contact and she could feel the evidence of a tightly leashed desire pressing impressively against her stomach.

The evidence that he did indeed want her made her bold and she tangled her tongue with his, responding to his kiss with an abandon she'd never known she was capable of.

She'd spent so many years repressing her sexual desires, they rushed through her now with the power of a California wildfire.

She moaned, moving against him, needing more than the kiss, but too involved in it to do anything about that.

As if he could read her mind, Zahir's hands began exploring her body through the thin silk of the wedding *galabeya*. He traced the embroidery along her spine, sending raptures through her body.

When his hands cupped her bottom, she could not suppress a needy whimper. An approving growl came from deep in his chest as he lifted her to press the apex of her thighs against his hardness.

Her legs spread of their own volition, but the skirt of the long Arabic gown constricted how far she could do so. He didn't seem to mind, making another sound of approval as he intimately thrust against her. The contact between them, even through the layers of silk of their clothing, sent electric sparks exploding along her nerve endings. His thrusts became more urgent as she felt warm moisture develop between her legs.

How could this feel so good? How could she feel so out of control already? They weren't even naked yet.

He tilted her pelvis just so and suddenly sensation unlike anything she'd ever known was making her womb clench. She mashed her mouth against his, needing to be closer.

He gave her what she needed, taking their kiss into something wildly carnal.

Unfamiliar tension built inside her, pleasure tinged by almost panic at the unfamiliarity of it, made her body shake even as she pressed against him in wanton need for something she couldn't give name to.

And then it came, that nameless something, a supernova of sensation that made her body go rigid as she cried out against his mouth. A sob built in her throat as the pleasure burst, and ebbed, and burst again.

She couldn't breathe. She couldn't think. She could only feel and that was too much. Too intense and yet she never wanted it to end.

But something this immense had to end, or kill her. She was sure of it.

Her heart felt ready to explode from her chest. If this is what he could do to her with a kiss, she was never going to survive what was to come.

The jolts of pleasure grew farther apart as her body ebbed toward relaxation more and more until she was completely limp against him. Her grasp on his neck nothing more than a caress, really, as her muscles certainly weren't supporting her.

Finally, breaking the kiss, he swung her high against his chest and smiled down at her. "You are amazing."

She could not speak to respond, merely shook

her head. He was the incredible one, playing her boldly like a sitar's strings.

"Making love to you will be my greatest pleasure." She forgave him the smug tones edging his voice.

They were well-earned. Besides, his words weren't smug at all. He could have said it would be *her* greatest pleasure, and they both knew that would be the case.

She was a virgin after all.

Making the other claim was a sop to her feelings that she could not help loving him for. Tonight would definitely not be the beginning of her learning to suppress that love like she always had her feminine sensuality.

That would come later, when she was not in his arms, experiencing feelings and emotions beyond comprehension.

Even so, she wanted to ask if he meant it, but knew that would be a very stupid thing to do in the circumstances. A negative answer was so not what she wanted to hear right now. Still, she could not help giving him a doubtful look.

His expression turned intensely serious as he carefully laid her on the huge bed. "You are the only woman I have ever touched that has been mine alone. You cannot know what satisfaction that gives me."

She wanted to call him a chauvinist. Tell him he was arrogant beyond belief. But most of all, she wanted to ask what he meant. Of course, Elsa would not have been untouched when Zahir began seeing her; his former mistress would have had liaisons with other men.

Angele didn't do any of that, though, because for the first time in all the years she had known this man, a glimmer of vulnerability showed through his supercontrolled exterior.

"All yours." For tonight.

His teeth flashed in another sensual smile. "All mine."

If he sounded like he was making a permanent claim, she convinced herself it was simply her ears hearing what they craved. Not a truth that resonated in her heart.

"You will make love to me now?" she asked softly.

"I have been making love to you since you stepped into my room."

She did not question it. She certainly could not deny it.

He began to undress, pulling back the layers that named him crown sheikh of his people until he stood before her in the soft glow of a hundred candles, his perfect body completely open to her gaze.

Skin a shade darker than hers covered bulging muscles she would not have expected in a man who spent his days playing politician. She'd always known he was strong, but now she believed the rumors that none of the security force in the palace could best him on the sparring mat.

"You look like an ancient Bedouin warrior."

"A man cannot be weak and lead his people."

"I have never questioned your mental stamina."

"You mean you *have* questioned my physical prowess?" he asked and then laughed, the sound free and full of genuine amusement.

That laugh was as much a gift as the pleasure he drew so unnervingly from her body.

She choked on her own amusement. "Of course not, I just…"

Her eyes could not help devouring him with hungry need. He was so incredibly masculine, his hardened sex standing out from his body in impressive splendor.

"I think you like looking."

"I think I do, too."

"You sound surprised."

"I don't make it a habit of looking at naked men."

There was that laughter again and she could not even mind it was at her expense. "I should hope not."

"It suddenly occurs to me that I'm debilitatingly naive for a woman from my adopted country." She doubted there was a single woman who worked on the fashion magazine that employed her as an editorial assistant that was as innocent to sexual things as Angele.

"You are exactly as you should be."

She knew he meant it, but she could not help thinking that if she'd been a bit more experienced, perhaps he would not have found Elsa such a fascination.

She dismissed the thought as unnecessary and destructive. Elsa Bosch was not here, was not even in Zahir's life any longer. Angele was. For now. And at this moment in time, that was all that mattered.

"I think I could stand here and let you look and you would come from that alone."

"Arrogant."

He shrugged. "Perhaps, but you cannot know what a pleasure it is to have those doe-soft brown eyes eating me up like the tastiest dessert at the feast."

"I doubt there is another man alive who I would

find more appealing." She didn't mind telling him the truth.

Tonight was not for self-protection. That started tomorrow. When she flew back to the States, no longer a virgin and no longer the promised future bride to the heir to the throne of Zohra.

"Naturally."

She laughed again, her heart tripping in her chest at his obvious desire to be seen as the best in her eyes. "Naturally."

"No other woman can compare to you lying on my bed as you are."

Wearing his grandmother's *galabeya*, he meant, looking like the bride she would never be. But surprisingly the thought did not make her sad, but rather brought a smile to her face. "You've never brought another woman in here, have you?"

"Of course not."

"You're living out your teen fantasies, aren't you?" she teased.

He shook his head. "They're much more recent than that."

She opened her mouth to say something else, but he reached down and caressed his shaft with a sure hand. She gasped. She wanted to be doing that.

"All in good time," he said as if reading her mind.

Then he stepped forward until he stood against the bed. "It's time to undress my bride."

It wasn't a real wedding night, but he was going to make it as close to one as possible for her. And she was going to let him.

She wasn't surprised when his first action was to remove the slippers on her feet, but it shocked her speechless when he leaned down to take each foot into his hand and place a soft, sensuous kiss on the arch. He didn't stop there, either, but caressed her feet, pressing points that seemed directly linked to the empty ache inside her.

She was moaning and clenching her thighs by the time he'd moved his attention to her calves.

"Such soft, silky skin, but I know a place you will be softer."

Her breath came in harsh pants and she shook her head.

"I assure you, you are. Soft, delicious and wet."

Delicious? Did he mean…but her thoughts splintered as he pushed her gown up to expose her thighs to his gaze and that talented mouth.

Words gasped out of her without meanings as she discovered that her inner thighs were far more sensitive than she'd ever realized.

He chuckled, the sound wicked and delicious. "Are you sure it is the right time to be praying, *ya habibti*?"

"I…what? It…"

That smile that told her he was about to do something naughty creased his sensual mouth. Then, he pushed her *galabeya* higher and suddenly stopped, letting out a deep sigh of clear approval. "Oh, this is nice."

"You like my panties."

"Oh, yes, *ya habibti,* very much." He stroked

a single finger right over her clitoris and pressed down into the silk.

She jolted, arching her body toward that teasing touch.

"I do like these, but I am going to adore what is underneath them."

"You are so much earthier than I ever expected."

"I told you, I am a traditional man of my people. We celebrate the delight of pleasure."

"Your Bedouin tribes, perhaps."

"You would be surprised."

Maybe she would be. Like Jawhar, Zohra was one of the few Arabic countries whose outlook and culture had always suffered less religious oppressions than their surrounding neighbors or the rest of Eastern Europe.

"I'll take your word for it."

"You should not have to." It was the first time he had outright criticized her upbringing in America rather than Jawhar.

"So, show me now." She wasn't about to

get into a discussion on that particular topic right now.

"Oh, I fully intend to." And he did, caressing her until she was in a fever pitch of desire.

She wasn't sure how it happened, but she lost the *galabeya*. Finally. He took a moment to admire her in her lacy bra before removing it. He paid the kind of homage to her breasts that felt almost spiritual, but at the same time was very, very carnal.

Her nipples were aching and her panties literally soaked before he pulled back to ask, "Are you ready for me?"

"I've been ready." She'd meant to yell it out, but her voice was gone it was a barely there croak.

"I also."

But still, he took his time removing her wet panties. And then, instead of covering her with his body like she expected, he pressed her thighs wide apart and began to touch her with careful, knowing fingers.

"Zahir," she pleaded.

"It will be easier for you if I deal with your maidenhead with my fingers."

"What?" she gasped in a shocked whisper. And then shook her head frantically. "No. I… That's…"

But his forefinger and middle finger were already pressing inside, pushing against the barrier that stood between her virginity and their ultimate connection. He rubbed gently, making circles with his fingertips, pressing, pressing… always pressing.

It was a dull ache, not a stabbing sting. The small pain helped bring her to a more alert awareness as Zahir started his preparation of her body for his penetration.

"You are so careful with me," she breathed.

He gave her that smug half smile that she found more endearing than annoying. "Naturally."

"Is it a learned trait, or bred into you, I wonder?"

"What?" he asked, but his knowing gray gaze said he had the answer already.

"Your arrogance."

"You have met my father. It is genetic."

Yes, she knew the king of Zohra as well as the King of her father's country, Jawhar, and she would have to concede the point. Supreme confidence was definitely a family trait.

"Khalil and Amir do not seem quite so over the top with it."

"I am not sure Grace or Jade would agree with you but, *aziz,* you should not be thinking of other men while I am doing this." He pressed against her clitoris with his thumb and all thoughts of arrogance and his family flew from her brain.

A long, low moan snaked out of her throat as pleasure intensified in that one spot and then radiated outward. He continued the pressure massage against the thin barrier while caressing her sweet spot with his thumb in a way guaranteed to make her forget her own name.

She felt the stunning ecstasy begin to build again, this time all the more intense for knowing what it would lead to. Her body went rigid with tension, the dull ache inside her drowned in the hurricane of desire.

As the pleasure exploded he pressed through the barrier, her pleasure muting the sting of pain. She still felt it, but somehow it was natural, a moment meant only for them.

He looked into her eyes, his own so dark they appeared black. "Now, I make you mine."

She didn't reply. Could not form words to deny the claim and refused to face the truth of its temporary nature.

There was no need for her to respond as he moved between her legs, his engorged, steel-like hardness pushing inside her.

She could feel the stretch as her most intimate flesh strained to accommodate his. His member was much thicker than his fingers had been inside her. The sensation of not only being joined to him, but completely filled by him washed over her.

Neither spoke as he rocked gently with his hips, pressing deeper with each small thrust. Their gazes remained locked, the connection something so much more than physical. But then, she'd never expected anything else.

She loved this man with her whole heart and sharing her body with him was both spiritual and highly emotional.

Despite the obvious need making his muscles bulge from the tension of holding back, Zahir leaned down and placed the gentlest of kisses on her lips.

Tears washed her eyes, but she wasn't ashamed of them. They seemed an appropriate reaction to this moment. He did not seemed fazed by them, either, merely tilting his lips at one corner as he brushed the moisture away with his thumb.

"Are you ready?"

She almost asked for what, but he shifted just that much and she felt a new type of pleasure. Something so intimate and primal that she could do nothing but nod.

He did not smile, though she could sense his satisfaction at her agreement. He did begin to move, starting a careful, steady rhythm that was at once wonderful and not enough.

"More, please, Zahir."

He shook his head; the strain around his eyes the only indication that holding back was taking its toll on him. "Not this time. You are too new to this. You will have nothing but pleasure from me this night."

"It *does* feel good," she said somewhere between pleading and affirmation.

And they didn't have a *some other time* between them.

Rather than answer, he kissed her again, but this time with an unrestrained carnality that revealed how close to losing his control he really was. She responded, losing herself in the joy of their connection.

His movements grew jerky, though he did not let himself go as she was craving. A small voice in the back of her head told her she would thank him for his control later, but right now, she was once again reaching for the pinnacle of pleasure.

When it came, it washed over her in a warm wave unlike the frantic convulsions of the first time. However, his body seized, muscles straining, his neck corded as he threw his head back and let out a primal shout of completion.

A sense of accomplishment washed over her, adding to her happiness. She had given him this, just as he had given her unimaginable pleasure.

"It is done." His voice held a profundity that touched her deeply.

No matter the cause, she and Zahir had been one for this moment in time.

She wanted to say something, but tiredness overtook her and she felt the room fading even as Zahir whispered words of praise next to her ear, their bodies still joined.

CHAPTER FOUR

ZAHIR lowered himself and Angele into the steaming, fragrant water of the bath. Worthy of communal baths anywhere in Zohra, the traditional mosaic tiled rectangular bath could easily accommodate four adults. It would only ever serve him and Angele however.

As her toes touched the water, she began to stir.

The soft lighting was brighter than the candlelight in the bedroom, but not so bright it should hurt her eyes. Nevertheless, he bent protectively over her as she wakened. He'd never had a lover fall into dozing like she had, a picture of perfect peace and contentment.

It had stirred something inside him he did not want to examine too closely.

"It smells so good," she whispered as she

snuggled her head into the joint of his shoulder and neck.

A small bag of fragrant herbs floated on the surface near them. He had added the vial of specially prepared oils to the steaming water as well. "It is the traditional bathing treatment for after the wedding night."

"For all of Zohra, or for your family?"

"These herbs and spices are mixed only for the royal family." He brushed his hands down her stomach, tempted to go lower, but refrained. She needed time to recover before he made love to her again. "They are supposed to help assuage the aches and pains post coitus."

"They're doing a bang-up job." The husky tone of her voice challenged his intentions further.

"I am glad you find it so."

"Don't you?" she asked, as if daring him to deny the lovemaking had not been impacting for him as well.

He had no desire to attempt such a falsehood. "I do."

Though he suspected he found the bath slightly more reinvigorating than she did. He could not imagine a more pleasing wedding night. The marriage would have to be organized and dignitaries from all over the world invited, but he had no intention of maintaining chastity with her between times.

He could even be grateful they had this time to explore their sensual relationship without concern of the next heir's conception. He wondered what form of birth control she had decided on, but did not feel tonight was the one to discuss such mundane matters.

Tomorrow would be soon enough.

Angele was intelligent and highly organized. He had no doubt whatever option she'd chosen it was the best and most reliable on the market. When she planned something, she did it with a thoroughness that impressed even his father, or so the king had told Zahir.

He felt honored she had planned this time for them, no matter what nerves had prompted it.

"Your en suite is huge. Is that a royal thing or a rich thing?"

"It is a Zahir thing." He spent his life serving his people. When he got an opportunity to relax, he wanted to be able to do so in absolute comfort.

"I suspected, but well…it's not as if I've ever gone into my parents' en suite or my uncle's, for that matter."

"You have refused to live in your parents' home since their reconciliation."

"It happened when I was an adult." She paused as if thinking of the past. "It was time for me to get my own place anyway."

"Had you been raised in Jawhar, you would have remained with your parents until our marriage."

She tensed, but her tone was even as she said, "But I was not raised in Jawhar."

"No, you were not."

"Does that bother you?"

"No." While he found her independence somewhat disconcerting, he found he liked the woman floating in his arms.

"You've made a couple of comments that implied it did."

"Mere observations on differences are not an accusation of unacceptability."

"Sometimes, they feel like they are."

"Feelings are not fact."

"True."

"Emotions cannot be trusted." That reality had been drilled into him from childhood as he trained from his earliest memory to take over leadership of the kingdom of Zohra.

"Perhaps that is true sometimes, Zahir, but the lack of emotion can be just as bad."

"To control one's emotions is to control the negotiation."

She sat up, unexpectedly sliding away from him in the water. "All of life is not a political negotiation." She settled on the underwater bench opposite, her gaze searching, her expression earnest. "Don't tell me you use those tactics when dealing with your family?"

"Not telling you would not make it any less true."

Her lovely brown eyes widened and then narrowed. "You mean that."

"I do not make it habit to lie."

"You hid your relationship with Elsa Bosch for years." An expression of chagrin came over Angele's features before she bit her lip, clearly wishing she had not said that.

Nevertheless, he would answer the implication. "I kept it private. This is a necessary survival tactic for those of us who spend the majority of our lives in the public eye."

"Discretion is minimal, subterfuge preferred," she said quoting something he knew his uncle often said.

"Sometimes subterfuge is necessary, but that does not make me a liar."

She looked away, her brows drawn together,

but then she sighed. "So, you treat your parents like competing world leaders?"

While it was hardly a subtle way for her to change the subject, he did not call her on it. He had no desire to discuss one of the major mistakes of his life.

"My father especially. I successfully negotiated for my first horse." He smiled at the memory. "I lost the negotiation for a private family-only birthday party when I was ten, though."

"You were shy?"

"Timidity is not an acceptable trait in a world leader."

"You were ten."

"Nevertheless, I was not shy."

"Then why no other children?"

"That option was not on the table for negotiation."

Her brow wrinkled charmingly. "I don't understand."

"I lobbied for a party with my siblings. My father insisted on a state dinner."

Her gasp was far too adorable. Perhaps even he could be influenced by the emotion of the moment the first night with his bride.

"You mean you weren't allowed to have a children's party at all?"

He shrugged and admitted, "I was seven when I had my last children's party."

He had continued to try to negotiate for one until his twelfth year, when his father had informed him he was a man and had to put away childish things. It was the way of things for someone in his position. He knew his cousin in Jawhar had been raised with a similar set of ideals.

"That is terrible."

He shook his head. "You are too softhearted."

"No child of mine would be forced to have a state dinner for his birthday celebration." She sounded like she was discussing some form of torture.

And he could not help chuckling. "I learned the importance of my role and responsibilities."

It had been an effective lesson in putting the needs of his people before his personal desires.

"You learned that you were not allowed to be a child." Her tone implied she had just discovered something of importance about him. "It wasn't the same for your brothers."

"Naturally not."

She glided back toward him through the water. "Tonight, no one else is here. This is not about duty and obligation."

Suddenly a stricken expression took over her features. So, she remembered she had made this night a condition of the ridiculous "offer" she had made to let him out of their families' agreement.

He was tempted to let her flounder simply because the entire premise to this night was so very ludicrous.

However, she was right. "Making love to you in no way feels like a duty."

Her gaze searched his, as if trying to ascertain the truth of his statement. He knew she would find what she sought. For he spoke the truth.

Which was something of a relief for him, though he would never admit it.

The brilliance of her smile was worth his admission. "Tonight you are simply Zahir, not Crown Sheikh."

He was never anything less than what he was, leader and servant to his people. Not even during his time with Elsa, though for those stolen hours he had come closest to being simply a man than any other.

It was not a thing Angele could comprehend. Even had she been raised among their people. To know from birth that an entire country depended on you for its well-being was a circumstance known by only a handful in the entire world. And from those he had met, he knew not all were raised from infancy with the sense of responsibility to their people that his father and mentors had instilled in Zahir.

He would not shatter Angele's beliefs however and they were not entirely false. While not the entire truth, either. This night, he *was* as far removed from his position as dutiful sheikh as he could allow himself to be.

Fully cognizant he needed to make the night special so Angele would lose her fear of intimacy between them, there was still no denying that making love to her in this way—without the benefit of an official wedding—was not the action of a dutiful, responsible sheikh of his people. An internal voice, that sounded suspiciously like one of his mentors, chided him. Telling him there were other ways he could have allayed Angele's fears.

The simple truth, as unexpected as it had been to realize, was that Zahir *wanted* Angele. He found her more sexually desirable than he'd ever allowed himself to realize. The years they had waited to formalize their engagement, much less marry, had taken a toll on him as well. Though he had not known it.

He had forced himself never to think of her sexually. At first, because she had been so young and later because that part of his psyche was reserved for Elsa.

He now accepted that Angele was the ideal woman to share his bed and had been all along.

He pulled her back into his arms. "Are you ready to continue this night out of time?"

Her doe-soft eyes darkened with desire and she nodded before angling her head in a clear invitation to kiss.

It was an invitation he would never reject again.

Angele woke to pleasurable, never before experienced aches in her body. No doubt the pain would be acute but for the two soaking baths Zahir had insisted she share with him the night before.

A night filled with more passion and pleasure than she had ever thought possible.

The temptation to ask him to maintain their status quo as promised for future marriage was so strong, she'd literally had to bite her tongue to keep it back as they said their goodbyes in the wee hours of morning.

Though she would have much preferred waking in Zahir's arms at least one time in her life, she understood his concern with the possibility their tryst would be discovered if she did not leave while all but the security men on duty slept. So, she had gone, her body sated and her heart filled with longing for what would never be.

Although she had showered with Zahir before leaving his rooms, she took another bracing one in semicool water now. She needed every trick to maintain her resolve.

She packed quickly, leaving out the four envelopes she had prepared before stepping foot in Zohra.

One held a letter to her pseudouncle, the King of Jawhar telling him she was backing out of the agreement to marry Zahir sometime in the distant future. She apologized, pleaded with him not to hold her father accountable for her choices and told him she would understand if he no longer recognized her as part of his family. Her heart would have broken at the prospect, but it had shattered all those months ago when she'd first seen evidence of Zahir's affection for Elsa Bosch and there wasn't anything left to break.

Or so she told herself.

The second envelope was similar to the first, only the letter inside was written to Zahir's father. In this one she once again apologized and begged the king to consider her actions her own and in no way a reflection on her pseudouncle or her own parents—as none were aware of her growing discontent with the agreement as it stood.

The third envelope was thicker. It contained a letter to Zahir, this one the only one she had written this morning. She thanked him for their one special night and told him she would never forget it.

She also explained about the enclosed pictures, detailing when she had first received them and how. She gave him as much information regarding the blackmail as she could, including a list of payments she had made and how she had done so. She assured him she had told no one, not even her parents of the pictures or the blackmail monies she had paid.

She hoped he would discover how best to keep them out of circulation, for his sake as well as his family's. But come tomorrow, or perhaps even tonight, the blackmailer would know that Angele was no longer a pony in this race.

Her eyes flicked to the final envelope, the one that would ensure there would be no turning back. Though, really, it was only symbolic. It held a press release, scotching any "rumors" of a suspected permanent connection between the house of Jawhar and the house of Zohra vis-à-vis a marriage between her and Zahir. She had included a couple of personal quotes. One to the effect that she had no desire to live her life in the public eye as a royal and the other her absolute refusal to make a permanent home outside of her adopted country, America.

After reading it, her father might disown her and her mother would undoubtedly be furious, but Angele wasn't going to live the rest of her life without love. She just wasn't.

She might not be American by birth, but she'd been raised around an entirely different set of ideals to the duty-bound royals that led Jawhar and Zohra. While she loved the country of her birth and Zohra as well, at heart? She was a modern American woman.

She wasn't about to allow Zahir to be forced into a marriage he so clearly had never really wanted, either.

She was under no illusions. He would probably enter another arranged contract, but this time he was older. Zahir would have more input into who his chosen bride was to be. Angele could only hope, for his sake, that it was someone he *could* develop real feelings for.

She snuck down the secret passageways for the last time and left Zahir's packet in his room while she knew he was busy with his father. She left each of the letters to the kings with their respective secretarial staff. And finally she dropped the press release off with the PR department.

She had prepared a timed email with a duplicate release to be sent to the major news distribution agencies in a few hours. She would be in flight back to the United States when news hit.

Cowardly? Perhaps, but she preferred to think of it as politic.

Back in the U.S., her denial of a connection to the House of Zohra would constitute little more than a blip in the plethora of social news about drunk-driving celebrities and irresponsible megaconglomerates destroying ecosystems.

Once she was in the car headed to the airport, she pulled out her phone to make the most difficult call of her life. Her parents would not be pleased.

Refusing to take the easy route, she called her father first. That conversation went much as expected, but when he blamed her mother for insisting Angele be raised in the United States, she'd had enough.

"Had you managed to keep it in your pants, I would have grown up in Jawhar. Don't you dare blame Mom for this."

His outraged gasp at her crassness had no problem translating across the cellular connection.

"In point of fact, it was your ongoing infidelity that convinced me marriage to Zahir would never work," Angele added. "I will not put myself in the position of living as Mom did."

"She never wanted for anything."

"If you really believe that, then you've learned nothing despite your change in behavior."

"You do not speak to me with such disrespect, Angele."

"The truth is not disrespect." He couldn't even accuse her of a snarky tone, because her voice was as devoid of emotion as her heart right now.

She preferred the dead feeling to the pain that was sure to come as her final separation from Zahir sank in completely.

"Your mother and my relationship is not your business."

"I agree, but that does not change the fact that your example is one I absolutely refuse to follow."

"Zahir is not a hot-blooded man." The words *like myself* were implied but not said.

Angele wasn't about to tell her father just how wrong he was. After the previous night, though, Angele knew the truth. And the certainty that Zahir had spent similar nights with Elsa Bosch managed to pierce her numbness with a hurt that Angele chose to ignore.

So much for a decimated heart having no capacity for further pain.

"You cannot do this, Angele."

"It's done."

"We will discuss this further later." The royals of Zohra and Jawhar had nothing on her father for arrogance. "Right now, I am to meet Malik and Faruq. I am sure you and I both can guess the planned topic of our conversation."

"You are not listening, though why that should surprise me, I have no idea."

"Angele!" The shocked way he said her name spoke volumes.

"Please, Father. I love you, but I don't want to live my mother's life. I simply won't. I delivered letters to both kings with my stated intentions and apologies before leaving the palace."

"Leaving the…where are you?" For the first time, her father's voice sounded worried rather than angry.

The car pulled up outside the airport. She got out without answering her father, or waiting for the driver to open her door.

Once her luggage was on the curb, she said, "I'm on my way home."

"Your home is here."

"It never has been and it never will be." She sighed, ignoring the twinge in her heart the words caused her. "Please listen to me, Father. I included a copy of the press release I sent out to the major news agencies with the letters I delivered to the kings. Your meeting would be best spent deciding how to deal with the PR ramifications of my decision than trying to determine how to change my mind."

"Of course we will change your mind."

"No, you won't."

"Damn it, I changed my whole lifestyle to ensure this wedding would one day take place. You will not derail that in a fit of feminine pique."

"What are you talking about?"

"Surely Zahir told you about the little talk we had several years ago. He's always been your hero." Her father's tone implied he'd neither enjoyed the *little talk* nor the fact he'd lost his place as Angele's hero.

Tough. He was entirely responsible for both she was sure. And yet, she heard herself saying, "I'm sorry."

Though why he should think Zahir would have told her about the discussion was beyond her. Before this wedding feast, the time she and Zahir had spent together alone could be measured in minutes, not hours.

It was her father's turn to sigh. "Zahir informed me that he would not marry a woman whose father made headlines in the scandal rags on a regular basis."

She had no problem believing that. Zahir's near rabid protection of the family name and reputation of the royal house was well-known.

"So, you turned faithful…" She paused, swallowing down bile. She'd thought he'd done it to save their relationship and that had hurt enough, as she'd so wanted him to do it for her mother's sake. To learn he'd done it to earn a more entrenched place in the royal house just made her sick. "Or at least *circumspect,* in order to make sure your daughter married into the Royal House of Zohra."

"Faithful," her father bit out. "I realized my actions were doing all harm and no good. Certainly they never had the effect I had hoped."

"You hoped sleeping around would have some

kind of positive impact?" she asked with patent disbelief.

"Your mother refused to get pregnant again. I accused her of becoming pregnant with you only to trap me into marriage to begin with." A long drawn-out pause followed. "She never denied it."

"Was this before, or after you had your first affair?" What was she asking? Her brain and mouth were connected without a filter in there somewhere.

"It does not matter."

"I'm sure it did to Mom."

"She would not even try to give me a son."

"I am sorry to have been such a disappointment to you." And she'd never even known she had been.

"That is not what I meant."

Strangely she believed him. Her father hadn't ever done anything to make her feel like he had wished she'd been a boy. "I thought you didn't care if you had an heir since you aren't actual royalty."

"You know our people, though you were not raised full-time among them."

And in the culture of his homeland, to have no son to leave his name and worldly possessions was a great tragedy.

"I'm sorry," she said again, feeling her father's pain across the distance between them.

She understood the dynamics of her parents' marriage a little better, but she still had no desire to emulate it. "Mom loves you. She always has."

"I know that now." For the first time since their initial greeting, her father's voice held a measure of contentment. "I say again, Zahir is not me. He will not make my mistakes."

Memories of the photos she had left in Zahir's room rose to taunt Angele as she pulled her rolling case to the private plane security checkpoint. Even so, she did not reveal to her father that Zahir was no lily-white duty-bound sheikh, no matter what everyone else believed.

"I can't marry him, Father."

"You must."

"No."

"These are just prewedding jitters."

"We aren't even officially engaged." *Sheesh.* "This is me being smart enough to avoid a future that holds no appeal for me."

"It's a future you are imagining, not the one that will be."

"Have you always loved Mom?" she asked instead of answering.

The answer was immediate and without doubt. "Yes."

"And still you hurt her for years, as she apparently hurt you as well." Angele understood now it had gone both ways, but that certainly did not give her more hope for her own future. "If you two, loving each other, could do so much emotional damage, how much worse in a marriage that only one person feels love?"

"Zahir is not a man to love." Her father's instant answer without even pausing for thought to consider which of them felt that love was another brick in the wall Angele was trying so hard to build around her heart.

"My flight is leaving in a few minutes."

"You are not leaving Zohra."

She heard the threat in her father's voice, but she ignored it. She'd taken precautions to make sure she could and would leave today. She'd finagled a spot on a private plane headed to the States. So, even if the commercial flights were grounded while the royal guard searched for her, she would be going. Even so, she had timed her call to her father so that it would take a miracle for her flight to be discovered and stopped in time.

"Please, accept it. The press release has already gone out."

"We can say it is a hoax."

"I'll do a live interview."

"You will not."

She would do whatever it took to stand by her decision and let her silence tell him so.

Her father cursed fluently in Arabic. "Malik will disown our friendship."

"He's not that vindictive."

"It is a matter of pride."

"Yours. If it was all that important to either of the kings, one, or both of them, would have pressed for an official date before now. The agreement has been in place for a decade."

"You have only been an adult for five of those years."

"Half a decade."

"They are pressing for it now," he said, rather than argue the point.

Very typical for her father. Focus on the now, on the positive and ignore everything else.

She wasn't so sanguine and never had been. "It's too late."

Her father cursed again and she winced. She had known this conversation would be hard, but had foolishly thought herself immune to her father's disapproval.

"I love you, Father. I hope you'll be able to forgive me one day."

She hung up before he could say anything more.

She went through VIP customs, barely registering the words spoken to her or those she used in reply. Her heart ached. Whoever said emotions are felt in the head had never been in love. Her chest felt tight, like any second her heart was just going to give up and stop beating.

No matter what she'd said in her letters or on the phone to her father, walking away from Zahir was the hardest, most painful thing she'd ever done.

Last night had been the most amazing experience of her life, but then she'd looked at those pictures again and she knew. No matter how good a lover Zahir might be, he didn't love her. Only right now, she almost thought living with him without his love would be better than living without him at all.

She forced her feet to move forward, to climb

the stairs to the private jet. The owner said something to her. She replied, but couldn't remember what either said as she buckled herself into her seat. She did remember pleading a headache, glad when that seemed to buy her the silence and privacy she needed.

She didn't know the retired statesman or his wife very well and they appeared content to keep themselves to themselves. As far as they knew, they were doing a favor for the Royal House of Zohra, but they clearly didn't expect conversation.

For which she was grateful, rather than offended. She wasn't up to it. It was taking all her strength to stay in her seat and not return to the palace and a passel of angry royals.

The captain had just announced he would be taxiing into position for takeoff shortly when Angele's mother's number showed on the screen of her phone. She turned it off as the engines warmed up.

Nothing productive could come from her talking to her mom right now. And her call with her father had been difficult enough.

Angele's mother's love and approval had always been freely given. The prospect that breaking the contract with the royal family of Zohra might change that was not an outcome she felt emotionally ready to deal with.

CHAPTER FIVE

His body beneath his robes of state rigid with shock, Zahir stared at his father. Replaying the words Faruq had spoken in his mind did not aid in making sense of them.

Angele would not have done this. She could not have done this. Not after their *very* successful night together.

"You did not expect this," Faruq said with some censure.

No, Zahir had bloody well not expected anything like this. Not after last night. Especially after last night. But betrayal and shock were choking him, anger their close bedfellow, so he merely shook his head.

"Her leave taking, these letters…" Faruq wasn't sounding like a father, but a disappointed king. "It all implies forethought and planning."

"It's one of her talents." Zahir allowed with heavy irony to mask his growing fury.

His gazed jumped from his father's grave expression to matching looks on the two other men in the king's private study. King Malik's frown was two parts anger, one part confusion. Cemal appeared resigned, though clearly not happy.

That attitude of resignation bothered Zahir more than he wanted to admit, feeding the anger he was doing his best to keep under control. "Did you know about this?" he asked the older man.

"No." Cemal did not elaborate, but King Malik was more than willing to fill in the gaps. "She called him on her way to the airport."

"And we were unable to stop her flight?" Zahir asked, knowing full well how feudal he sounded and really, not caring.

"She cut the timing too fine and left on the private jet owned by one of the wedding guests."

Zahir cursed.

"She outwitted us," King Malik said with some admiration.

Zahir did not comment, but reached out in a silent demand to see the letter his father still held. He was not so impressed right now by Angele's superb attention to detail.

Faruq passed the papers over. "She included a copy of her press release as well—it denies rumors of your possible betrothal."

"You're serious?" Zahir asked in an angry disbelief he was unable to entirely quash.

There was being thorough and there was being outrageously stubborn.

Faruq nodded grimly. "According to her letter, it won't go live for a few hours."

"She did not want us blindsided by the announcement," King Malik said.

Blindsided? After the night they had spent in his bed, how could Zahir be anything but? He scanned the pages in his hand. "Like hell she does not wish to live in Zohra. She loves it here."

Both kings nodded their agreement, though it was King Malik that spoke. "That has always been my understanding."

"She chose the excuse most likely to lose her favor with the people of Zohra and Jawhar while increasing Zahir's sympathy with them." It was the first time since Zahir had entered his father's study that Cemal had offered anything more than a monosyllabic answer to a question. "It is the equivalent of her falling on her sword."

The words conjured up Angele's claims she would not allow herself or Zahir to be railroaded into marriage, and her subsequent promise to take the blame in the media and with the royal families. He'd convinced himself she didn't mean it. Clearly he'd been spectacularly wrong regarding her motives for their "wedding night."

Not in the least comfortable with an image of himself as being so weak he needed such protections, the fury inside Zahir went from simmer to full boil. He was not that man. That she could not see that truth infuriated him, but like always, he kept his emotions under tight control.

"The fact she broke the engagement was

enough of a sympathy vote for me," Zahir said with cold sarcasm.

Cemal shook his head. "Not if she gave her true reason for doing so, which I've no doubt she did to you."

Zahir remembered the conversation he'd had with his intended only three nights ago, words he had dismissed as nerves. "You believe she spoke to me of this?" He shook the papers in his hand, his grip so tight they wrinkled.

He wasn't denying it, but he wasn't admitting anything, either.

"I know my daughter. She does not take the easy way out."

"That is why she called our engagement off with a letter," Zahir mocked.

How had she considered it unnecessary to speak to him personally? Had she thought her illogical claims in his study that night to be sufficient final word on their future?

If she did, it only showed how very little she

truly understood the man who she would one day marry.

Cemal wasn't buying it. "She called me and I'm confident she spoke directly to you."

"Did she?" Faruq demanded of his son.

Zahir gave a jerk of his head. Regardless of whether he accepted that conversation as definitive word on the subject, obviously Angele had seen things differently. He ignored a curiously sharp pain in the vicinity of his heart at her easy dismissal.

"And you did not feel it politic to warn me, or her uncle?" Zahir's father demanded, his own anger blatant and no distant relation to the emotionless facade he had always demanded of Zahir.

"*Adopted* uncle," Cemal stressed, once again entering the discussion. "And it's not an *engagement*. Their relationship was never formalized. Not in ten years."

"We all know the reasons behind that," Zahir said.

"Camel dung." Cemal made no attempt to

hide his disgust. "You could have announced the formal engagement anytime, but you chose not to and my daughter got tired of waiting."

"So, she thought to force my son's hand with this?" Faruq asked in a deadly quiet voice.

Zahir's father had taught him to negotiate, to manipulate and to retaliate. The man hated being on the receiving end of circumstances and manipulations out of his control.

Cemal's expression turned even stonier than it had been as he'd voiced his accusation of Zahir's neglect over his duty. No, he hadn't labeled it as such, but each man in this room knew who was responsible for the ten-year-long "understanding."

"On the contrary," Cemal said, his voice just as cold as Zahir's father's had been. "This is my daughter making sure nothing can force her into honoring a contract she believes would sow nothing but unhappiness for her future."

"That is ridiculous, *my brother*," King Malik said, laying his own stress on the family claim along with a conciliatory hand on Cemal's shoulder. "The girl is in love with Zahir and always has been. It's as easy to read every time she is near him as the most basic of primary books."

Zahir grimaced. "A woman in love does not break off an engage—" At Cemal's narrowed eyes, Zahir amended his words to, "a *contractual promise* for future marriage."

"She does if she believes her love will never be returned."

Zahir wasn't going there. "She is no starry-eyed teenager to expect flowers and poetry from a marriage such as ours."

"I think you are missing the point here," Cemal said. *"There isn't going to be any marriage."*

"And this pleases you?" Zahir accused, stunned by the possibility. He was no man's idea of a poor son-in-law choice.

"Not at all, but I know my daughter well enough to know that once she sets a course of action, she sticks to it."

Zahir didn't disagree. Cemal and Lou-Belia

had wanted Angele to attend finishing school in Paris rather than university in the States. Angele had gotten her degree from Cornell. Neither had approved her decision to get her own apartment, but Angele had lived on her own since her sophomore year at university.

Zahir had never given much thought to what he considered Angele's minor rebellions, particularly when he had approved her choices both times. He had not wanted her to marry him without having had a chance to live at least something of a normal life.

Now, he thought he'd been a fool to encourage the blatant independence. Had he spent more time getting to know her, he would have realized what such choices might wrought.

"We can put out our own press release saying hers was a hoax, perpetrated by our enemies," King Malik suggested.

Cemal shook his head. "She threatened to do a live interview if we did that."

So, Cemal had tried to dissuade his daughter from her intended path.

And all Zahir could concentrate on was the truth that such persuasion should not have been necessary after the previous night. Those hours out of time fed Zahir's anger and an unfamiliar tightness in his chest.

"So, we have no choice," Faruq said with a worried glance at his son.

Zahir was no object of pity or concern and never would be. "There is always a choice. We will release our own statement."

"And what will it say?" King Malik asked, hope gleaming in eyes reflecting a lifetime of power and even less tolerance for not getting his own way as Zahir's father.

"That I recognize waiting so long to announce our formal engagement was a mistake. I will woo my bride-to-be. The country can expect announcement of my formal betrothal by the end of the year."

If hearts and flowers were what she wanted,

then they were what he would give his errant bride-to-be.

His father's bark of laughter was tinged with no less disbelief than Angele's actions had sparked. King Malik and Cemal merely stared at Zahir as if he'd taken leave of his senses.

"You doubt my ability to woo one innocent woman after witnessing my skills at negotiations with world leaders?" he demanded.

Cemal coughed. "A woman is not a world power."

"No, but one day your daughter will be married to one." Zahir bowed his leave-taking to his father and King Malik, inclining his head to Cemal. "If you will excuse me, I have a campaign to plan."

If fury drove him more than desire, that was his own business.

His father frowned, but said, "If you are sure this is the course of action you want to take, I will have the press release with your apology and intentions drawn up and disseminated."

"Do you have another suggestion?"

"You could let her go."

"I cannot. In waiting too long to finalize our engagement, I failed Angele. I will not do so again through inaction." Besides, they had already had their wedding night.

There would damn well be a wedding.

"Good luck," Cemal said, sounding like he meant it.

King Malik nodded. "My staff and family are at your disposal. I will have my wife create a dossier most likely to help you in your cause." King Malik turned to Cemal. "She will draw upon Lou-Belia's knowledge of her daughter as well."

Cemal nodded. "Good. Her mother knows Angele better than anyone else."

"Thank you." Not that Zahir doubted his ability to convince Angele to marry him.

However he would take what help was offered. After all, he had been certain that after the previous night she would never have gone through with this farce of denying him to begin with.

He understood his intended's motivations a thousandfold better several hours later. He'd finally returned to his rooms only to find a thick envelope with his name on it and stamped with a red Private prominently in several places.

The letter was somewhat illuminating, but coupled with the pictures, Zahir realized he was damn lucky Angele had handled breaking the contract the way she had. Acknowledging that did nothing to improve his black mood.

The fury he'd felt at her defection was nothing compared to the incendiary rage he experienced knowing she had been subjected to blackmail.

Looking through the pictures, he had no doubts about who had taken them and used them for monetary gain, either. There could only be one person. Only Zahir had thought Elsa too smart to risk something like this. She stood to lose far more than she could ever hope to gain.

Regardless of who the culprit was, though,

Angele should have brought the problem directly to him. Instead she had paid the money.

They were not close, but she had to have known that he would deal with the problem.

The fact Angele had paid money to keep his name out of the tabloids boggled his mind. It simply was not the way things were done. She had to have known he would have safeguards in place in just such an event.

She certainly expected him to be able to take care of it now, or so her letter suggested.

Nevertheless, her loyal, if foolish, actions were further indication that she was indeed in love with him. Or believed herself to be. He gave very little credence to love and all it entailed, but her feelings for him should make his wooing a simple matter.

A little voice amidst all his anger reminded him that he'd thought his seduction and lovemaking would have prevented her leaving in the first place. His father wanted to know why not just let her go?

It was simple really. Zahir didn't lose. Ever.

Equally as important, Zahir accepted that he owed his future bride a courtship. He was furious with her, but his own inaction in regard to their betrothal and ill-advised relationship with Elsa had driven Angele to her recent actions.

Zahir had failed in his duty to her and that was worse than losing. That was a blow to his integrity he simply would not accept.

First, he had to handle Elsa and her threats. She must be made to understand that Angele was and forever would be off-limits.

Then Zahir would go after his reluctant bride.

Sitting at her desk at the magazine, Angele read the article her mother had sent her the link for. Confusion slowly morphed to sheer, unadulterated anger.

That arrogant idiot.

Even after seeing the pictures she'd been sent, Zahir thought he could convince her to go through with the wedding contract. Did he have no idea how hopeless that belief should be?

Apparently not.

He was quoted as saying he'd been neglectful and planned to rectify that. Really? When? After all, she'd been home for two weeks and he'd not so much as called her in all that time.

Typical.

A couple of days ago, she'd received a short note, in his own handwriting. It had stated that the "picture problem" had been taken care of and that he hoped to see her soon. Like that made everything better. The excitement she'd felt at seeing the return address on the stationery, quickly followed by her disappointment there hadn't been anything more personal in the short missive, and then the tiny curl of hope at his professed desire to see her soon had made her mad.

And disgusted with herself.

Almost as disgusted as she was with him right now.

What really had her blood pressure rising was his statement his countrymen could expect announcement of a wedding date by the end of the year.

Not merely the formal engagement, but the actual *wedding date*.

If she'd been reading a printed newspaper she could have thrown it down. Would have thrown it right into the garbage. As it was, all she could do was glare at her computer monitor while a growingly familiar nausea rolled over her in a clammy wave.

She was sprinting for the bathroom moments later, anger at Zahir vying for supremacy at upset at her own colossal stupidity.

Zahir arrived at the magazine's offices late Friday afternoon, six weeks after Angele had left Zohra. He was in search of the woman he had spent far too many sleepless nights thinking about over the past weeks.

It was his guilt at putting his duty off that kept

him awake. He wasn't happy that his inaction had led to the need for this dramatic wooing.

He liked the fact his and her names had featured prominently in the media since she'd felt the need to back out of the contract even less. First, speculation on her motives and then his reaction had kept the gossips busy. Then reaction to his own press release had been flurried and florid.

Finally the long-distance wooing he'd done while preparing his offices for his absence had sparked several articles and numerous requests for interviews. He'd turned them all down—well, all but one. However, he'd allowed details of the gifts he'd showered his fiancée-to-be with to leak.

A woman deserved others to know she was appreciated and Zahir was doing his best to express that appreciation for Angele. It had taken a while, a couple of weeks in fact, for his fury at her defection to simmer down to the point he could focus on wooing rather than reading his errant bride-to-be the riot act. He was proud that none of the short notes accompanying his gifts and flowers held any sort of recriminations in them.

He'd even agreed to do an interview and photo spread for her magazine. He'd allowed the magazine's photographer into his offices at the palace in Zohra and agreed to pictures both in his robes of state and wearing designer suits custom tailored to his tall frame for the fashion magazine's feature article.

His every overture, including that one, had been met with a frustrating silence.

Now that his schedule was cleared, the time had come to step up his game.

Accompanied by his personal bodyguard and security detail and dressed in his best Armani and over robes of his office, Zahir carried a bouquet of yellow jasmine into Angele's office building. The receptionist looked up, her eyes going wide as he approached the large half-moon shaped desk in the center of the large lobby.

Giving one of his practiced political smiles, he asked, "Can you direct me to Angele bin Cemal al Jawhar's office?"

The young woman's eyes went even wider as she scrambled for some papers she nearly knocked from her desk, without looking away from Zahir and his security men. "Um…I don't… let me just make a call."

She scrabbled for her phone, her cheeks going a rosy-pink. She dialed and then started speaking rapidly almost immediately.

"Yes, there's a…I mean I think he's a sheikh, or something. I don't think he's dangerous, but he's got these scary-looking men with him. He's looked for Angele. I think it's Angele anyway. He called her Bin-something, but we've only got one Angele, right? I mean, there's an Angie in accounting, but no one else called Angele…"

He could hear the sound of someone speaking on the other end of the line, the deep tones indicated a male, but Zahir could not be sure.

"Yes. Oh, probably. He's carrying a bouquet of

those exotic flowers Angele's been passing out to whoever would take them over the past few weeks."

Zahir's brows drew together as the implications of the receptionists words sank in. Angele had been disposing of the flowers he sent her by giving them away to all and sundry? What had she done with the jewelry, then? Pawned it?

His annoyance must have shown on his face because the receptionist flinched and the papers she'd managed to save went sweeping to the floor. It was probably a good thing she wore an earpiece for the phone, or the receiver probably would have gotten dropped as well.

Zahir took a step back from the desk as he schooled his features into impassivity.

The receptionist was nodding at whatever she was hearing over the phone, though she hadn't said anything for several seconds.

She jumped. "Um…yes, of course I was listening. I'll call her extension. Right now, sir."

The flustered woman pressed a button and

then three more. "Um…Angele? Well, yes, I did mean to dial your extension. It's just there's a man down here that looks like, well he could be dangerous, or something, but he's got flowers." The woman turned away, making some effort to whisper, though her words were still clear. "You're sure he's not dangerous?"

Zahir managed to keep the scowl he felt off his features, but it was a close thing.

"All right. I'll tell him you'll be down shortly. It will be shortly, won't it?"

Apparently even Angele's patience had worn thin with the young woman because there was clearly no reply. The receptionist looked up and then flinched, her face blanching as she must have realized he could hear every word she'd spoken.

"Uh…Angele said she'll be down soon. You can…you should probably wait for her over there." The young woman waved toward some chairs by the window on the far side of the large lobby. Zahir nodded stiffly and led his security detail to the other side of the lobby.

"Hello, Zahir."

He turned at the sound of Angele's voice, his smile of greeting sliding right into a concerned frown.

Her usually honey-gold skin was wan and she had circles under her eyes not hidden by her makeup. She also looked like she'd lost weight; her pale cheeks were hollow.

"Are you well?" he asked and then could have bitten his own tongue. He knew better than to make queries of this type in a public place.

"I'm fine." She smoothed her hand down the front of her sheath dress.

The color of eggplant, the dark purple was usually a complimentary color for her, but today it only served to enhance the washed-out tone of her skin. Nevertheless, she wore it with stylish élan, her accessories and hair as well put together as any of the models her magazine photographed.

Regardless, she really had no business being at

work if she was not feeling well. She needed to be home in bed, being pampered and coddled. His plans for the evening took a sudden shift.

"It is good to see you." Bowing slightly, he offered her the bouquet of yellow jasmine.

She simply shook her head, making no effort to take the flowers. "I'm cleared to leave. Did you have a destination in mind for this conversation?"

There was something off about Angele's attitude, but he had no time to ponder it as she turned and began walking toward the front doors. He handed the flowers off to one of the security guards to deal with. And then, he caught up to Angele with his longer strides and they exited the building together.

His limousine waited by the curb. She headed toward it without hesitation. Bemused by her assertive and frankly, unexpectedly cooperative behavior, he followed.

They were in the limo when she turned to him and asked, "Where are we going?"

"We have reservations at Chez Alene." But he did not think they should keep them.

"My favorite restaurant."

"I am aware."

"My mother?" she asked.

"Ultimately, yes."

"Ultimately?"

"Uncle Malik believed I needed assistance in my plan to woo you."

"Let me guess, he had the queen compile a dossier." There was nothing in Angele's tone to indicate how she felt about that, one way or the other.

"Yes."

She nodded, making no comment on the fact they had known each other their whole lives and a dossier of that type should not be necessary.

"You gave away the flowers I sent you?" he asked.

"Yes."

"Might I inquire why?" He wasn't sure he wanted to know what she had done with the jewelry, or the designer bags and shoes he'd had her mother pick out for her.

"Why did you send them?"

"You deserved a proper wooing after my years of neglect."

"Duty then."

He opened his mouth to deny it, but could he without dishonesty? Not completely. "Perhaps, to an extent. However, they were also a reminder that you were in my thoughts even separated by the miles."

"Poetic."

He shrugged. "What can I say? I am a man of my culture."

"You're a pragmatist with a terrifying ability to gauge human nature and use your observations to best effect."

"You do not believe me sincere?"

"I believe you were thinking of me, but we both know the reason for that, and it didn't have a thing to do with some romantic longing to see me."

"Define romance. Our last night together was not so forgettable."

Her hand settled against her stomach and she frowned. "No, it really wasn't."

"That bothers you."

She sighed, looking out the tinted windows at the traffic surrounding them. "It doesn't matter."

"I assure you, it does."

"No, it really doesn't."

"I know you think—"

"Look, let's just stop this politically motivated seduction, all right?" Despite her confident words—if possible, she looked even more fragile and out of sorts than before. "It's a waste of both our time and your efforts."

"You are so certain I cannot sway your mind?"

"You don't need to. If you agree to certain conditions, I will marry you."

CHAPTER SIX

ZAHIR waited for Angele to take the words back, or at the very least, enumerate these said conditions. But she simply stared off into space, breathing shallowly.

"This is unexpected," he said finally when it became apparent she had nothing else to add.

In fact, he was so stunned his usually facile brain had the speed of cold honey in processing her immediate capitulation.

"Disappointed?"

Oddly he was. And not a little bit wary as well.

"I am aware you love me," he said, feeling his way in a blind negotiation he had not expected in any form at this stage. "I still believed your pride too wounded to make our reconciliation an easy one."

She laughed humorlessly. "You believe I'm agreeing to marry you because I love you?"

"Why else?" The prospect she had suddenly decided to submit to duty was not the comfortable thought it should be.

"We didn't use condoms that night."

His brow wrinkled as he tried to catch her point. "So?"

"So." She rolled her eyes and waved at her stomach as if that was answer enough.

His brain had no trouble catching up this time and the implication stole all the air from his lungs.

"Surely you were on the pill, or some other form of birth control. You planned the night well ahead of time." He'd been certain of that during their night together and even more convinced after seeing her letters to the kings and polished press release she'd left behind.

"Yes, I planned it. No, I didn't go on the pill as part of my preparations." Self-loathing laced her voice. "I should have…I realize that now."

"Why the hell not?" he demanded, his voice raised in a way he never allowed.

"I don't know. It wasn't rational. I know that, but I thought…one night. I was a virgin, disgustingly naive. I wouldn't get pregnant." She frowned. "I thought you'd use condoms."

He ignored the last statement and concentrated on the ones that came before it. "You are too smart for that."

She glared at him and then seemed to deflate. "Yes, I am. There's no excuse. I really just thought…I don't know. I've tried to understand why I didn't say anything when you didn't use a condom, but my excuses are feeble and stupid. Even to me."

"You expected me to use condoms?" He couldn't dismiss the claim a second time.

Her brow furrowed as if she didn't understand his question. "Well, yes."

"Why?"

"Why not? We weren't lovers. For all intents

and purposes, what we had was a one-night stand."

"What we had was a premature wedding night," he practically shouted and then took a deep breath in shock at himself.

She waved her hand in dismissal, apparently unmoved by his loss of cool. "Call it what you like, but I expected you to use condoms and when you didn't… Well, that first time, I was just so lost to the moment and afterward, I thought the damage was already done."

"Damage is right."

That brought the glare back, but there was something else in her expression, something he couldn't quite name. "What is your problem? You're getting your way."

"You think this is me getting my way? My first child has been conceived without the benefit of a wedding ceremony. I have spent my entire life protecting my family from scandal and now it will visit itself on my child. He or she will forever carry the stigma."

"Please. This isn't the Middle Ages."

"If this child is my heir, his throne could be called into question." He cursed, using more than one language and feeling like that still was not enough to express his fury at the current development.

"Do a DNA test."

He drew himself up and scowled. "I do not doubt his paternity."

"I know that." She rolled her eyes. "I meant so there could be no question of the baby's parentage to others. Anyway, it might be a girl."

"Yes, because the men in my family are so good at fathering female offspring." They hadn't done so in five generations that he knew of, not in his direct lineage anyway.

She turned an interesting shade of green and started taking more rapid shallow breaths.

"Are you well?" What the hell was he asking? She was pregnant. Of course she was not well.

"Morning sickness," she gasped between breaths.

"It is nowhere near morning."

"The baby doesn't seem to care."

"This is not acceptable."

She cringed, her expression filling with too many emotions to name. "You don't want the baby?"

"Of course, I want this child. How could you ask such a thing?"

"Well, you're acting like it's the end of the world, or something."

"Are you that naive?"

"I am not naive. Not anymore."

"I disagree. You have not considered the complications this pregnancy will cause. It will be all over the press. After a lifetime of protecting my privacy and behaving with circumspection, I will make a bigger tabloid splash than your father and my brother combined."

"You don't want me to have this child? You think I should terminate my pregnancy?"

"Have you lost your mind?" How had she gone from what he had said to something so reprehensible? "Do not ever suggest such a thing to me again."

"I wasn't suggesting it. I'm not the one having a temperamental fit."

The accusation snapped the last thread of his control.

"Did you do this on purpose?" he leaned forward and asked, memories of Elsa's betrayals freshly branded in his brain. "Was this your way of getting back at me for my relationship with Elsa?"

"Now, who's making insane accusations?"

"Women scorned have been known to do worse."

"You never scorned me, you arrogant ass!" Then she swallowed convulsively and scrabbled for the button that would open the sunroof.

He reached up and pressed it when she seemed unable to make the stretch. "When you were eighteen, and I refused your kiss."

"That was five years ago."

"Revenge is a dish best served cold."

She took several deep breaths before saying, "I can't believe this."

"Join my world."

"Oh, get over yourself."

Fresh air came in through the opening in the roof and Angele leaned back in her seat, seemingly breathing easier. Good.

He mentally ran through a list of things needed doing. Consulting an eminent obstetrician was top of the list. "You are not taking this seriously, what this pregnancy means."

"Oh, I'm taking it seriously all right. I know exactly what it means."

"Oh?" She certainly had not shown proper understanding so far.

"Yes." She shot daggers with her usually doe-soft eyes. "It means I'm agreeing to a marriage I don't want."

"Why?"

"Why what?" she asked, sounding genuinely confused.

"Why agree to the marriage?"

"Because I'm not a stone-cold bitch."

"I never said you were."

"My mother told me something a few years ago. It was after I found out about my father's infidelities. I apologized to her for having to live in the States where I could know relative anonymity, instead of her home country of Brazil where she was better known. She'd done it to protect me."

"I am aware."

"Well, she told me I had nothing to apologize for, that from the moment a baby is conceived, his or her needs must come first."

"You are willing to marry me for the sake of our child."

"Under certain conditions, yes."

The limo pulled to a stop.

She looked at him with that same sick expression she'd had before opening the sunroof. "We're not at the restaurant. We're hours too early for dinner."

She swallowed convulsively on the word dinner.

"No, we are at your apartment building. I originally had planned to give you time to get ready for our date."

"More like, you intended to seduce me before dinner and hoped to cement the romantic proposal over dessert." The words should have been mocking, but she merely sounded resigned.

"You think you know me." She was wrong. On the proposal over dessert part.

He'd planned to woo her in person for two weeks before popping the question, so to speak.

"What?" she asked. "It would have been a good plan, if unsuccessful."

"You do not think I could seduce you?"

"I'm positive you could. Even feeling like my stomach is a jumping board for little green men right now, but I still wouldn't have said yes to your proposal."

"But you will now, because of the pregnancy."

"Neither of us has a choice. This baby deserves

better than to be shunted to the side as the unacknowledged offspring to a future king."

"I would never refuse to acknowledge my child."

"You know what I mean."

"No, in fact, I do not."

"Never mind. This arguing is making me even more nauseated than usual."

The sickly pallor to her skin lent truth to her claim. He mentally shook himself. Now was not the time for recriminations. What was done, was done.

He had been right earlier; she clearly needed taking care of.

"Then we will not argue."

"Thank you." She sighed again, letting her eyes close as she seemed to concentrate on her breathing.

When the driver opened the door, Zahir wasted no time exiting and then leaning back inside to help Angele alight from the car. Once she'd cleared the vehicle, he bent and lifted her into his arms.

She gasped. "What are you doing?"

Flashbulbs went off and he knew this picture would show up in the media sooner than later.

"I am caring for you. You clearly need looking after."

"The papers are going to have a field day with speculation accompanying those shots."

"They'll have more than enough juicy tidbits of truth to publish over the next weeks."

"We're not going public with the…" She looked around and closed her mouth.

He carried her toward the building allowing his bodyguard to go inside first and the rest of the detail to bring up their rear. "These things have a way of making it to the light. Better to announce the happy event than scramble to respond when some tabloid does."

She let her head fall onto his shoulder. "I don't want to."

"We will talk about it later," he said in his

newly formed determination not to cause her stress with further disagreements.

Angele sat at the bistro-style table in her kitchen and watched with bemusement as Zahir efficiently prepared a pot of peppermint tea.

"You are awfully comfortable in the kitchen for a Crown Prince," she observed, happy to focus on anything but recent revelations.

She'd done a lot of facing reality and growing up over the past weeks. Realizing she was pregnant at all, but much less with the probable heir to the Zohrian throne, was all the catalyst she'd needed to shed the last of her naiveté. She'd been shocked by her own joy, even in the face of all this pregnancy would mean.

Like she'd told Zahir, the baby came first, but more than that, she already loved her child and always would.

Angele would do what needed doing to make sure her child's life was all it should be, but that didn't mean she wanted to talk about it right then. She was just starting to feel something other than nauseated.

Zahir shrugged as he finished pouring the boiling water through the infuser into the teapot. "According to my mother, the inability to do something as basic as make a cup of tea is the mark of laziness rather than wealth."

"I'm sure Lou-Belia would agree with her."

"Your mother is an imminently sensible woman."

"You think it sensible to stay with a man who chose infidelity over argument in the attempt to convince her to have another child?" she asked, curiosity rather than bitterness in her voice.

Between discovering she was pregnant and accepting the inevitable consequences that would have for her life, Angele had come to terms with a lot of things. Her present required all her energy; she didn't have any left over to dwell on her family's past.

Zahir carried the teapot and two mugs to the small wrought-iron table. "Life is what it is."

"I think I'm finally learning what that really means."

"She chose what she considered the lesser of two evils." Zahir's tone said he knew what that felt like.

In his position, she would be surprised if he didn't. Nevertheless, Angele warned, "It's not a choice I would make."

"You cannot doubt that things are completely over between Elsa and me."

"No, but there are other Elsas in this world."

"I have no interest in them."

"I hope that's true."

"You doubt my word?" Zahir's shock was almost comical.

She poured the tea, adding a scant teaspoon of sugar to hers. "Not exactly."

"Then what, *exactly?*"

"The future. I doubt the future."

"Well, don't."

She wanted to laugh, but simply shook her head. "If only it were that easy."

"It can be."

"Certain safeguards would make it easier."

"The conditions."

"Yes, my conditions."

"For you to marry me, despite the fact you carry my child." He stirred not one, but three teaspoons of sugar into his tea.

She'd always found his sweet tooth endearing, something she knew about him that few people noticed. Because he didn't eat desserts. But he did drink cocoa and put lots of sugar in his coffee and tea. Seeing evidence of that sweet tooth now brought a measure of comfort, a reminder that not everything had changed.

He was still the same man she'd fallen in love with from afar, the same man she'd planned for most of her adult life to marry.

"Yes."

"I'm not going to like them, am I?"

"No." There was no point in sugarcoating it—no matter how much he might like sweet things, but she wasn't going to feel guilty for trying for some semblance of assurance for her future, either.

She might not be that naive, year on from university woman who believed she could have a one-night stand with the man she loved and come out of it relatively unscathed, but she still had to have some level of hope for her future. His agreement to her conditions would give her that.

He sat back, his mug in one hand, his eyes fixed on her with that patented intensity of his. "I am all ears."

She took a deep breath and went for broke. "I want a prenup that guarantees me the right to raise our children in the United States in the event you take a lover."

She waited for the explosion, but none came. He simply sat, sipping his tea in silence and looking completely unperturbed.

"Nothing to say?"

"I assume there is more since you said *conditions* plural, not condition in the singular."

"Yes." Was he really as sanguine as he appeared? "I mean it."

"I assumed you did."

"You aren't angry."

"Considering your past, such a condition is hardly a shock."

"But…" He would never countenance his children being raised outside of Zohra. She finally stuttered as much out loud.

"Naturally not, but since it won't happen, I fail to see why I should become upset over your need for the reassurance on that score."

He was right, it *was* a reassurance. He might not maintain fidelity for her sake. However, she was wholly convinced that he would for the good of their children and the sake of the throne he protected so carefully.

Feeling light-headed with relief he'd accepted the first and she would have thought the *hardest* hurdle to overcome, she said, "I am glad you are not offended."

"I would be, if I believed your request was based on a lack of trust in me personally."

"You don't?"

"It's obvious that your past has a great deal of bearing on this, as I have said."

"And you do not think your ongoing relationship with Elsa figures into it all?"

"That was before we were formally engaged."

"You said you considered us as good as."

"In one respect that is true, just as in the same respect, a part of me already considers the throne of Zohra mine. However, it will not in actuality be until my father abdicates in my favor or sees his final days on earth."

"So, you did make a distinction." She was more thankful to hear that than she would ever admit to him.

"Do you not know me even that well?" he asked, sounding like he was finally feeling the offense she'd expected him to take earlier.

"I thought I did and then I got those pictures."

He winced. "Point taken."

"I realize now, I was hopelessly naive in my expectations, but those photos devastated me," she admitted.

She had no trouble reading his expression for once, it was pure dismay. "You believed I would be celibate once the contract was signed?"

"Yes." She felt foolish for that belief now. It had been a teen girl's fantasy she'd never reconsidered in the light of adulthood. At least, not until she'd been forced to. "You see, *I was.*"

"When I signed that contract, I was a twenty-four-year-old man. You were a thirteen-year-old girl."

"Are you saying it would not bother you if I had taken a lover since becoming an adult?"

He opened his mouth and then shut it again, no words emerging.

"Smart choice."

He frowned. "My initial response does not paint me in a favorable light."

"No doubt."

"Your other conditions," he prompted, clearly

not wishing to dwell on his unpalatable double standard.

"There are only two more."

"They are?"

"Your heir is allowed to have a childhood."

"I had a childhood."

"Until you were seven, yes I got that."

"I was not an unhappy child."

She was convinced that a man of Zahir's strength would have bloomed under any conditions, but she refused to allow her own children to face the same exact sort of childhood he'd been raised with. "This is not a negotiable point."

"You do realize that saying something like that to me is like waving the red flag to the bull?"

"I didn't—now I do."

"You wish to rephrase it?"

"No."

His brow rose in clear surprise.

"I am willing to marry you despite major personal misgivings for the sake of our unborn child. There is no point in doing so if being raised amidst the royal family of Zohra will be a source of unacceptable sacrifice and potential unhappiness for him."

"I told you, I was not unhappy."

"And I'm telling you, that heir to the throne, or a youngest daughter, it doesn't matter to me. My children will have the chance at a true childhood."

"As defined by you?"

"Ultimately, yes, but I am open to discussion on issues of importance to you."

"I will enjoy the challenge."

"Of course you will."

"Your final condition?"

This should be an easy one for him to accept, considering his own circumstances. "None of our children will have their marriages arranged for them."

"I acknowledge you are not as pleased with our arrangement as you were in the past, but that is no reason to dismiss centuries of tradition." A full measure of offense laced his voice and drew his spine ramrod straight.

"It's a tradition that should have disappeared with the Dark Ages."

"I disagree." If anything, his tone became more clipped. "The practice of arranging marriages is still common in the Middle East, parts of Asia and Eastern Europe. Just because you were raised in a different culture does not mean one is superior to the other."

"Your brothers are both happier because their marriages came about because of love rather than a contract."

"And my parents fell deeply in love after marrying because *their* parents arranged it."

"The risk of it not working out is too big."

"Love is no guarantee of happiness." He sighed. "Surely your parents' own marriage is enough to prove that to you, but if not—merely consider the divorce rate of your adopted country."

"I'm really surprised this is such a sticking point for you." This was the one condition she had believed he would accept without argument. "I would have thought that your own present circumstance enough to convince you."

"You were wrong." He said nothing more, simply staring at her with a bone-deep determination that she had no doubt carried sway at any table of negotiation.

But she couldn't back down about this. Zahir would never have been forced into marriage with her if not for that stupid contract. He would never have shown any interest in her and she would never have demanded that night in his bed.

The guilt she felt for doing so now was a big enough burden to carry. She couldn't bear to think of her own children having to submit to those kinds of circumstances.

She took a fortifying sip of tea, but he spoke before she got a chance to further her case. "I will offer this compromise."

She looked at him expectantly, waiting to hear what his supreme skills at negotiations would come up with.

"We will not force our children into an agreement."

"That's hardly a compromise. No one forced, or even cajoled you, for that matter. You signed that stupid contract out of duty and a sense of personal obligation."

"And I am not the one regretting that choice."

"You would be if Elsa hadn't slept around. You'd be wishing you could marry her right now."

"And if I had married her, even if she had been sexually faithful, I would have tied myself to a callous gold digger." He sounded like he considered that salvation from a fate worse than death. "The contract has been nothing but a boon in my life."

"That's why you looked at Amir with such envy at his wedding."

The shock on Zahir's features lasted less than two seconds, but it was enough for Angele to know he had not believed anyone had realized he harbored those feelings. "I expect to enjoy a relationship as fulfilling with you."

"I thought you made it a practice never to tell an outright falsehood."

"Eventually," he added, as if the word were pulled from him with rusty pliers.

She almost smiled. He was so intent on doing his duty, he would even create a hope for the future that had no basis in their current reality.

"But you do not believe love has any place in an agreement such as ours."

"We are getting off topic."

"Yes, we are. No arranged marriages for our children."

"I will agree not to press an arrangement on our children, but will not refuse to exercise my authority in conducting a negotiation on their behalf should they wish for me to do so."

She had a feeling that was as good as she was going to get on this point. "You absolutely promise to abide by the spirit, not simply the outlined terms on this point?"

"You are not a competing business or political interest. Believe it, or not, I do know the difference when it comes to family." Which was not a yes, but might actually be something even better.

It was acknowledgment that she, and their children, fell in a different category than other entities in his life. She might not have his love, but she would have a unique place in his life.

That would have to be enough.

CHAPTER SEVEN

ANGELE woke to the sound of Zahir talking in rapid-fire Arabic in the other room. He'd insisted she lie down while he took care of having dinner delivered.

A glance at the alarm clock beside her bed showed that a little over two hours had passed, startling her. She hadn't been sleeping well since returning from Zohra and had been positive she would not fall asleep when she'd acquiesced to Zahir's concern.

The man was far more adept at hovering than she would ever have suspected.

He didn't sound like a concerned husband-to-be right now, though; he sounded like a man who was brainstorming spin on the announcement of her pregnancy.

She surged to her feet, thankful the dizziness that had plagued her off and on for the past weeks was not showing itself. The need to pee, however, was. And no matter how urgently she wanted to speak with Zahir, it took precedence. She made a quick trip to the bathroom before going to find her stubborn fiancé.

His robes of office nowhere to be seen, his suit jacket and tie lying over the back of a nearby chair, Zahir sat on the sofa. An open laptop was on the coffee table in front of him, the screen showing a website dedicated to the care and feeding of pregnant women.

The indulgent smile that caused slipped right off her face as his words registered. He was still discussing how best to announce Angele's pregnancy, but now she knew who he was talking to. His father.

He'd told his father. Which meant her parents would know soon, if they didn't know already.

Her knees going weak, she stumbled to sit on the sofa.

Zahir jerked to face her, his expression going

concerned in a moment. He hung up faster than she'd ever heard him end a conversation with the man who was both father and king.

"Are you well?" He leaned toward her, examining her with all the intent of doctor on a house call. "I thought you would be better after a rest, but you are looking peaked."

"Thank you," she said with pure sarcasm. "Every woman wants to hear she looks like death warmed over."

"But I am concerned."

"Not so worried you hesitated to tell your father about my pregnancy though you knew I didn't want you to."

"It is a blessed event. Naturally I told him."

"That's not the way you reacted in the car." He hadn't seemed even remotely blessed then.

"I saw the potential problems first. It is in my nature." His tone was pure shrug even though his shoulders remained immobile.

She used to tease him about that trait. Right now, she found it more frustrating than funny.

"We also agreed in the car that we would wait to announce my pregnancy."

"Actually we were out of the limo when you expressed your opinion in that direction."

She made a sound of pure frustration at his attempt to tease around the issue. "You didn't argue with me." She took a deep breath and released it slowly, praying her earlier nausea would not return. "Silence is an implication of agreement."

"Clearly it is not."

"You knew I would assume you would wait to tell our families until we had spoken further about it."

"I did not tell your family."

"You think your father hesitated to share the news with King Malik and my father?"

Zahir shrugged, looking far from repentant. "It is good news worth sharing."

"You are a manipulator."

"I prefer master of circumstances."

"Call it what you like, I won't be tricked that way again."

"I did not trick you. I avoided unnecessary conflict so as to prevent further upset."

"I am upset now."

"Why?"

"I wanted to wait to tell *anyone*." She glared. "And I heard you—it's not just your family. You want to tell the world."

"I explained my viewpoint earlier."

"And that's it? We disagree and you do whatever you please?"

"Would it make you feel better if I claimed otherwise?"

"It would make me feel better if you said it and meant it."

"It will not always be as I wish it."

"Oh, really?"

"You left Zohra, did you not?"

"You're saying you would not have prevented me if you had been able to?" She made no attempt to temper her skepticism.

"You gave me no such opportunity."

"So?"

"So, you are intelligent and resourceful. I will not always get my way."

"I need to know that you won't act without thought to my feelings. I don't want a marriage based on a series of one-upmanship competitions."

"We are not children."

"Agreed."

"I did consider your feelings."

"And yet you still called your father with the news."

"Waiting to do so would only cause you further stress and upset. Prolonging a thing of this magnitude only invites more complications as it becomes more likely the opportunity to act on your own timetable will be taken away."

"No one knew I was pregnant until I told you."

"You have not been examined by a doctor?" he asked with clear censure.

She rolled her eyes. "Yes, of course, I have and everything is normal and as it should be."

"Good. I will expect the family physician to conduct his own exam however."

"I wouldn't expect anything else."

"So, this doctor knows that you carry my child."

"She knows I am pregnant, not who the father is and she is bound by laws of confidentiality."

"And you claim you are not naive."

"This isn't Zohra, Zahir. Dr. Shirley has no reason to believe the father of my child is a person of interest to the media. I'm hardly one of the glitterati myself."

"Perhaps that was once true, but things have changed since Amir's wedding."

That was putting it mildly. "You mean the very public courtship you were supposedly engaged in?"

"*Supposedly?*" he prompted, sounding none-too-pleased.

"I left Zohra six weeks ago. Today is the first time I have heard from you."

"I sent daily gifts for the past few weeks."

"Without a single phone call."

"This did not please you."

"Of course it didn't, but it didn't surprise me, either."

"I cannot claim the same. Your actions after our single night together astounded me."

"I told you my plans."

"I thought you were doubting the existence of passion between us."

"And when you gave me proof it existed, you assumed I would go forward with the plans to marry?" she asked, unable to hide her disbelief at his assumptions.

"Yes."

"You only hear what you want to hear."

"It is a failing."

"But not one you are often accused of."

"This is true."

"Yet, you don't deny it."

"How can I? Clearly, in this instance, I did hear what I deemed probable and acceptable."

"Lina walked away from the marriage arranged for her with your brother. What's improbable about that?"

"You are not Lina."

"No, I am not. She was raised with a much stricter sense of responsibility to her family's position."

"Lina was not in love with my brother."

Angele could not argue that point. Lina and Amir had barely known each other, despite growing up in the same circles.

"I see you do not deny loving me."

"What would be the point?"

"In the car, you intimated your feelings were not involved with your decision to marry me. It is only natural then to question if they have changed."

"My feelings for you were not a deciding factor in my decision to marry you. Our child's future was."

"Do you still love me?" he asked bluntly.

"Does it matter?"

"I prefer to know."

He'd been honest with her to this point, she could offer no less. "Yes, but I consider my love a detriment to this situation, if you must know."

"But of course it is not. Surely our life together will be eased because of it."

"You think I'll let you have your way because I love you?" she asked suspiciously.

"I am not that foolish, but it is my hope you will be content in our marriage because of it."

More likely it would cause her nothing but pain, but admitting that was just one step on the open and honest communication highway, her pride wasn't about to let her take.

The buzzer sounded and Angele gave Zahir a look meant to maim. "Two guesses who that is and the first one does not count."

"Dinner," he said with smug assurance.

She hoped he was right, because she was so

not up to playing happy families with her parents right now. She was still annoyed with her father for not giving her a heads-up on Zahir's plan to publicly court her. Angele had zero doubts Cemal had been in the know on that score, if not a major instigator.

And while her mother had said she'd forgiven Angele for breaking the contract, initially Lou-Belia had been hurt and very angry. They were talking again, but things were still a little stilted between them.

Zahir's bodyguard answered the summons from the doorman and then dispatched one of the security detail to retrieve their dinner.

One brow raised, Zahir smiled.

"Don't be so smug. They'll show up sooner than later."

"And you do not wish to see them? To share the happy news in person?"

"What part of *I don't want to tell anyone* isn't sticking with you, Zahir?"

He frowned, his eyes dark with disapproval. "It seems to me, you are the one regretting the advent of our child."

She opened her mouth to reply that of course she regretted becoming pregnant, but snapped it shut again on the words. Words, once spoken, could never be unsaid.

And she would never say such a thing about her baby, no matter the change in circumstances it brought to her life. The truth was, Angele had spent more years believing she would one day marry Zahir than the few months determined not to do so.

It was time to put her big girl panties on and deal with it. She was going to be Princess Angele bin Faruq al Zohra, and one day—God willing far into the future—she would be queen.

"No matter what the complications, I do not regret this baby." She pressed a hand to her stomach. "But I'm not up to presenting pure joy and celebration for my parents' sake, either. At the very least, I'm fighting a constant battle with nausea and an on-again-off-again vertigo that is truly disturbing."

He nodded, his handsome face set in lines of concentration. "I have been researching how best to treat morning sickness that has the poor manners not to confine itself to mornings."

"I've tried ginger and soda crackers. It helps a little, but I'm still not holding my food down."

"There are other options I read about. And according to our family physician, Vitamin B6 apparently helps a large percentage of women who suffer morning sickness. He also recommends acupressure wristbands used for antinausea as the result of motion sickness."

"I'm not sure I can hold a vitamin down long enough to do any good."

"There is also a combination medication that can be administered orally, or in a prepared hypodermic, but it can make you tired."

While that wouldn't thrill her, it had to be better than being sick. "I'll survive."

"It would make it difficult for you to do your job."

"Today was my last day." She'd given a month's notice soon after confirmation she was pregnant.

Shock widened his eyes. "You've already worked out your notice?"

"Yes."

"I expected argument about the need for you to leave your job."

"No."

"I see."

There would have been no point. It would be ridiculous for an editorial assistant to come to work with a bodyguard detail and she wasn't kidding herself. Angele knew that as soon as Zahir was made aware that she carried his child, security around her was going to be a 24/7 reality.

Besides, once they were married, she'd no

doubt they could and would visit the States often, but no way could she continue to live here.

"You reconciled yourself quickly to your changed circumstances," he mused.

"I had a lot of years to plan what our eventual marriage would require."

"This is true." He looked lost in thought for several moments and then asked, "So, you do not refuse to live in Zohra?"

"I only said that for the press release. While I will not pretend to have been raised there, or stifle who I am for the sake of conformity, I love Zohra. But I told you I wouldn't allow you to be blamed."

"I was very angry when I read that press release. I do not think I have ever been angrier in all my life." He said it so dispassionately that it would have been easy to dismiss his words as overkill.

Except for the look in his eyes. The color of molten metal, they shimmered with remembered rage at odds with the rest of his calm exterior.

She was beginning to realize that for all her hero worship of the man, she didn't know Zahir as well as she thought she had.

Seeing even a remnant of that furious reaction shocked her to her core and something told her it shouldn't. That she should have realized he would never see her defection the way she intended it to be taken.

Regardless, she wasn't completely buying the story he'd never been so mad. "Not even when you realized your former lover with a seriously questionable reputation was threatening to out your liaison to the press?"

The slightest movement that could have been a wince showed on his features when Angele said the words *seriously questionable reputation*, but other than that, Zahir didn't show any further emotion to the words. Certainly he didn't exhibit that latent anger he had in regard to Angele's actions.

"You knew it was Elsa?" he asked with just a

tinge of surprise. "Your letter was careful not to point fingers."

"I didn't know if you still cared for her." And she hadn't wanted him hurt any more than he would be by knowledge of the pictures and blackmail itself.

"She'll never attempt to hurt you again." The flat truth in his voice didn't allow Angele to doubt it.

She nodded. "I assumed you neutralized the threat to your good name."

"My name and reputation were a secondary consideration in this instance."

She found that hard to believe, but didn't call him on it. They had more important things to discuss. "So, when are we getting married?"

He didn't blink at the change in topic. "Since you are already six weeks along, there is no hope of a quick marriage stifling future rumors."

"Hence your insistence on announcing my pregnancy before our official engagement?"

"The announcement will be a joint affair."

"How lovely." The entire world would think he was marrying her because she carried his child and potential future heir.

But then, was that any different than the knowledge they were marrying as the result of a political contract between two kings? Probably not. It was her own fault that she'd always considered the other as less important because of her feelings for Zahir.

Talk about burying her head in the sand. "I'd make a fine ostrich," Angele muttered.

Zahir gave her a quizzical look, but she waved it off and said, "We could do something small fairly quickly."

Lou-Belia was going to pitch the fit of a lifetime when she realized her only child's wedding plans had to be rushed *and* scaled back.

"Small?" Zahir said the word as if doing so pained him. "For the Crown Sheikh of Zohra? I think not."

"Everything doesn't have to be done on a world leader scale." Really, really, it didn't.

Only the look on his face said it did. "Learn to accept the inevitability of it. We are political leaders, not celebrities to indulge in a secret ceremony on some private island. Our people will expect and deserve the opportunity to celebrate our joy with us."

"Not to mention assorted world leaders and their hangers-on," she grumbled as the reality of her change in circumstance began to make itself felt.

"It is inevitable."

"So, what do you suggest? I would prefer not to waddle down the aisle nine months pregnant."

"Be assured, it will not be that bad."

"How bad are you proposing it be?"

"You would be best past this nausea."

"Agreed." Fainting on her walk down the aisle was not the impression she wanted to leave with dignitaries and world leaders, much less her future family.

"We are in luck. Usually trying for any event of this magnitude with any less than an entire year of planning would be impossible. Two years would be preferable, but my father is hosting a summit to discuss world oil reserves in two months time. Were we to coordinate the wedding celebrations to coincide with the summit, the important political guests would already be in Zohra."

There was no room for sentimentality in that scenario, but she accepted that was her own fault. She couldn't help wondering if they had followed the contract and a regular schedule of engagement and marriage, if it would not have been the same, though.

"Our wedding is a political event." Which she'd known somewhere in the back of her mind, but had not really given thought to what that meant in the grand scheme of things.

She'd always looked at the Zohra-Jawhar connecting, never considering the further implications to her life.

Zahir was not one of his brothers. He was in

fact a Crown Sheikh, uncontested heir to the throne of both an oil and mineral rich country.

"I've really messed up, haven't I?"

He didn't deny it, but quoted another favorite Arabic proverb. One that was pretty much the equivalent of, *it is what it is.*

"For all my fantasies and daydreams, I never really considered what being married to *you* meant," she admitted.

"Had you attended finishing school rather than university, you would have had training in that regard."

She forced herself to remember what he'd said on their night together, that an observation was not a criticism. "But you supported my decision to go to university."

"I knew what marrying me would mean to you." Again, the shrug was in his voice rather than his shoulders.

"Wouldn't that make you even more determined I learn my future role?"

"I wanted you to have a chance at a normal life before we wed."

"But…" Unsure what she wanted to say, she let her voice trail off.

"My mother and aunt have both promised to mentor you in your new role."

"You've accomplished an awful lot in the two hours I slept." Not that she was surprised by that.

She did know him well enough to know how efficient he was and how very adept at making things work, whether it be a property rights negotiation or a family dinner. It had always been a pleasure to watch him finesse those around him.

She could hardly complain he was doing it to her now.

But he shook his head. "I made the request years ago, when you decided to go to university in America."

"It's no coincidence that every trip to Zohra and Jawhar in the past several years has included significant time with the queens." She'd been flattered, a little nervous and ultimately happy to spend time entertaining others with the respective women.

Though she would have traded that time for time with him in a heartbeat. That wasn't something she needed to admit to right now, though.

"No coincidence," he confirmed.

"I thought your mother was just getting to know me."

"She was, but she was also teaching by example and trying to share knowledge of your future life with you."

"Sneaky."

"I prefer subtle. I did not want you overwhelmed by the realities of what your life would be, though I wonder now if we were too subtle." His expression had gone contemplative. "You have too little understanding of what the role should and will mean for you."

She couldn't deny it, but it was still uncomfortable acknowledging that truth. "Maybe you didn't want me getting cold feet and backing out of the contract."

"Interestingly enough, I never once considered you would break the contract." He shrugged and said a word she was pretty sure meant *fool* in French.

"You are not a fool."

"I misjudged the character of two important women in my life."

CHAPTER EIGHT

"ARE you comparing me to Elsa?" Angele asked in a deceptively calm voice, while her temper stirred.

She'd made mistakes, but she was so cold-hearted that she would cheat on Zahir and then blithely try her hand at blackmail.

"Only in my false perceptions of you both, not your respective characters."

Still, Angele felt the need to say, "I did not betray you like she did."

He quoted another proverb, this one about seeing two sides of the same mountain leading to different impressions of the same thing. So, he read her attempt to walk away as a betrayal. She knew it had made him angry, because he'd admitted it. Understanding the source of that anger, only made it harder to know about.

Horrifically naive, maybe, but she hadn't meant to let him down.

She turned her head away, looking at the painting over her small fireplace. It was a cheerful impression of jazz musicians on the streets of New Orleans, done after the rebuild of the city. It always infused her with hope. Right now, all she felt was malaise.

Knowing how very deeply she had disappointed Zahir hurt. "I was protecting myself from a marriage without love, but I thought I was giving you your freedom, too."

"I accept that."

"But you don't accept it was a gift intended to benefit you." She had not been motivated entirely by beneficence, but she had wanted him to have a better chance at happiness, too.

She hadn't realized she'd been capable of hurting Zahir, but obviously, she'd been wrong. While his heart might not have been touched, she had dealt a serious blow to his pride and to his sense of honor.

Not to mention his trust in *her* integrity.

She sighed when he did not answer. "So, we somehow organize a momentous wedding while the world watches in two months time."

"Just so."

Apparently he was as willing to move their discussion forward as she was. There was simply no point in rehashing old arguments. Somehow, she would prove to him that she had his best interests at heart. And maybe, in the same space, she would learn to accept that he felt the same.

He'd certainly done his best to protect her and allow her what he thought she needed for happiness. Perhaps, in his mind, the years'-long wait had been as much for her benefit as his.

Moreover, he'd said repeatedly that he believed in fidelity in marriage. Making their engagement official would have required him breaking things off with Elsa. And while it hurt that he had not wanted to do so, Angele thought that Zahir had deserved his slice of happiness not related to his duty or role as future king.

Unfortunately for him, things had ended badly and unquestionably painfully.

If Angele could not be that moment out of time for him, she would show him she could be more. That she, Angele bin Cemal al Jawhar, could be a source of joy in his everyday life.

She would start now, by helping to plan the wedding with grace and as much enthusiasm as she could muster. "I think we need to call in the experts."

"A wedding planner? The PR department? Our palace event coordinator?" he asked while making notes on his phone.

"All of the above, I'm sure. But I was thinking the queens and my mother. Nobody throws a party like Lou-Belia."

Zahir paused and looked up, his gray gaze fixed on her. "I thought you did not wish to speak with your parents this evening."

"There's no point in putting it off." And some very good reasons not to, the chief among that Angele was not a naturally selfish person. "Mom will be hurt if I don't call her tonight, but we'll want to coordinate a conference call with her and the queens for tomorrow."

The buzzer sounded again.

"Impeccable timing," she said, putting on her game face and getting up to answer the summons, sure it was her parents showing up to share in the happy news.

Zahir's bodyguard beat her to it and Zahir asked, "Why do you always assume it is your mother when the buzzer sounds?"

"You honestly think King Malik has not already called my father?" she asked in response.

"Most assuredly, but are your parents not on the list of approved visitors for the doorman?"

"Of course, but it's policy for the doorman to buzz me to let me know I have visitors even if he doesn't need my approval to let them on the elevators."

"I see. It is very different than living in a royal palace."

"Yes, it is, but you've stayed in hotels."

"No one gets to me until they've been through at least two layers of security. There are no buzzers in my life."

Not sure he had been joking, Angele laughed anyway. They might have been raised as close as family, but their lives were entirely unrelated in so many ways.

A few moments later the door opened to reveal her obstetrician, not her parents.

Angele gasped as the older woman with salt-and-pepper hair cut in a short stylish look came into the living room. "You make house calls?"

Dr. Shirley gave Zahir a measured look before turning back to Angele. "In your case, I do, apparently."

"What did you do?" Angele demanded of Zahir.

"I did not conscript her, I assure you."

Dr. Shirley gave him another strange look. "No, he merely had someone in the White House give me a call and make the request."

"The White House?" Angele asked in a voice that nearly failed her.

"Yep, it even came up on my caller ID that way. Pretty crazy." Dr. Shirley sounded somewhere between annoyed and awed. "I've never been contacted by my local congressman, much less a White House lackey."

"What did he say?" Angele asked with unconcealed fascination. She'd never spoken to anyone from the White House, either, though she knew Zahir had attended State dinners there.

"That in the interest of Foreign Relations, I should consider making a personal call on you this evening."

"That's wild."

The other woman laughed. "I thought so, too. Apparently the father of your baby is quite worried about your ongoing nausea."

Worried enough to make a Federal case out of it, literally.

Angele stored away the warmth that made her

feel and said, "I thought we would look into the nausea medication tomorrow."

"Why wait?" Dr. Shirley said, tongue so obviously firmly in cheek. "I've got a prepared hypodermic in my bag."

"You're getting a kick out of this," Angele accused.

"Yes, I think I am."

Angele shook her head and then asked, "It won't hurt the baby? You're sure?"

"Absolutely not. I wouldn't give you anything that might harm your baby, but I'd like to try the acupressure band to begin with. If that doesn't work, there is an *acustimulation* device that is a step up, but it can cause minor skin irritation. And of course, I'd like to give you a shot of Vitamin B6 right now."

"Will that make me tired?" Angele asked, remembering her conversation with Zahir.

"No, though I recommend taking these sleeping pills in conjunction with Vitamin B6 at night before going to bed." Dr. Shirley handed Angele a familiar box. "They're approved for use during pregnancy and enhance the antinausea effects of the B6."

"When my mom takes those, she's usually pretty tired for a good part of the next day."

Dr. Shirley shrugged. "It happens. Depending on the dosage and your response to it, daytime sleepiness can result."

"I've got a lot of planning to do. I can't afford to be sleepy all day."

"Your health is of utmost importance." Zahir's tone brooked no argument.

Angele smiled at him. "Thank you for your concern." She turned back to the doctor. "I'd really prefer to try the other options first."

Right then, her stomach roiled and she had to turn away and swallow convulsively. Sometime soon would be good.

"I doubt it's much of a stretch to assume it's been a pretty hectic day for you," Dr. Shirley said. "I'd actually recommend you take the sleep aid tonight, and be grateful for the extra rest if it helps you nap tomorrow, too. From what you told me in my office at your last appointment, you haven't been getting much rest lately."

"I've had a lot on my mind."

"Considering who the father of your child is, I'm not surprised." The older woman reached out and squeezed Angele's shoulder comfortingly. "It isn't every day a woman finds herself making a family with an honest-to-goodness future king."

"I'm very honored." And she was, but overwhelmed was a word that fit as well.

"I'm sure you are, but you're also tired. And that's not good for you or baby."

"I had a nap earlier."

"You've still got a full set of luggage under those eyes," the doctor unapologetically pronounced.

Angele frowned at Zahir. "Why didn't you tell me I looked like a fright?"

"You do not look a fright, but I do recall telling you that you did not look rested."

Oh, right. "So, bags, huh?" she asked the doctor with a wince.

"Steamer trunks."

She gave a short laugh and sighed. "In the arm or the bum?"

"Let's go into the other room."

A stick in the bum then.

For the first time in weeks, Angele woke up feeling pretty good. No flulike symptoms, no urgent need to rush to the bathroom and throw up. She was still a little tired, but Angele would take that feeling over extreme nausea any day.

The bed beside her was empty. However, the rumpled pillow on the other side gave testament to the fact she hadn't spent the night alone.

Considering her ambivalent feelings toward their upcoming marriage, she should not enjoy that knowledge so much. But she did. Even though they had not woken together, knowing she and Zahir had spent the night in the same bed felt right.

Too right.

She'd been deluding herself to think she could really walk away from Zahir if he was determined to marry her. The baby made giving in easier, but the truth was, he would have eventually worn down her resistance. Because he had made it clear, he'd had no intention of giving up the future they planned together.

She just hoped neither of them would learn to regret that stubbornness.

Angele followed the scent of coffee to the kitchen and found Zahir and a dapperly dressed elderly gentleman with kind eyes sitting at the small table.

Both men rose as she came in.

Feeling better than she had in days, even with the smell of coffee and freshly cooked bacon in the air, she smiled. "Good morning, gentlemen."

Zahir introduced the older man as Dr. bin Habib, the physician to the royal family of Zohra.

"My O.B. was just here last night." She looked at Zahir. "How many doctors do I need?"

"Technically Dr. bin Habib is acting on behalf of the baby at this point. Though he will coordinate care with your obstetrician both here and when we return to Zohra."

"Please tell me you haven't tried to strong-arm Dr. Shirley into traveling to Zohra with me. I'm not her only patient."

"I have made no attempt to strong arm the honorable doctor."

There was something in his tone that made Angele look at Zahir askance.

The Crown Sheikh shrugged, doing a pretty poor job at casual regardless. "If I perhaps offered her a very persuasive remuneration package for doing so, that cannot be considered an attempt at coercion."

"Zahir!"

"What? You expect me to ignore your needs in favor of strangers."

"I'm sure there are perfectly competent O.B.s in Zohra." Though a small part of her was more than a little relieved she wouldn't be changing doctors.

"It is best to maintain continuity of care."

"She passed your background checks, then?" Angele couldn't help teasing.

She had no doubts that if Zahir had not considered Dr. Shirley the best of the best, no generous remuneration would have been offered.

"She is without equal."

"Did she accept your offer?"

"She did. She will travel with us to Zohra and then, barring any unforeseen complications, return monthly until your seventh month, at which time she will make her temporary home in the palace for the remaining duration of your pregnancy."

"You promise you did nothing to force her decision?"

"Such as?"

"Such as having the White House call her… again. Or her congressman or anything like that at all."

"I did not."

Angele nodded. As long as the choice had been Dr. Shirley's, Angele wasn't about to complain about something she wanted. "Any decaffeinated coffee on hand?"

"Naturally." Zahir poured her a cup from the carafe on the counter rather than the one on the table.

Dr. bin Habib bowed slightly. "I will remove to the living room while the princess partakes of her breakfast."

Angele didn't bother to argue that she wasn't actually in fact a princess. Yet. Instead she said, "I won't be long. I don't eat much in the mornings right now."

"I am sure you will find the nutritionally balanced menu to your liking," Zahir interjected.

She refrained from rolling her eyes and gave him a tight smile. "I'll do my best."

But she wasn't going to risk the debilitating nausea returning by eating too much, or something that might trigger it—no matter how good it was for her.

Zahir pulled out her chair and she sat down with a quiet, "Thank you," as the older doctor left the room.

Breakfast was, in fact both palatable and not overwhelming. Zahir kept the conversation light while she ate, waiting until she was finished to broach the subject of the wedding again. "I have arranged a conference call with our mothers and the queen of Jawhar, as well as the event coordinator for the royal palace."

Angele bit her tongue on the slightly sarcastic retort that first popped into her mind and said, "Great. What time?"

"Eleven this morning."

"Won't the event coordinator have gone home for the day at that point?"

"He will make himself available."

She supposed that for a man who considered himself on call to his position 24/7, asking an employee to stay late of an evening did not seem like an unreasonable request. "Okay. Mom will be over in about an hour."

She'd called her parents the night before, after getting the shot of Vitamin B6 and before taking the safe-for-pregnancy sleeping pill. Lou-Belia had been uncharacteristically calm when faced with the news of impending grandparenthood and the upcoming royal wedding. She'd agreed to come over in the morning, suggesting Angele get a good night's rest.

Angele couldn't help thinking that Zahir had somehow managed to contact her parents ahead of time and apprise them of his wishes to encourage her to get more sleep.

"Is your father coming also?"

"He is."

"It will be a busy day for you."

Angele didn't argue, but wondered if busy was a code for challenging, because she knew that was exactly what her day was shaping up to be. Not that Zahir's would not be equally difficult. He had to come up with a definitive plan to announce what many would say was scandalous news. He would be questioned and criticized.

The media was going to have a field day with the situation; the perfect prince had fallen from grace.

And it was her fault.

Knowing he had anticipated her being on the pill or some equally effective form of birth control added to her sense of guilt. Not that he couldn't have at least asked, but *she'd* known for a fact they weren't using anything.

"What is that look?" he asked, his brows drawn together in a concerned frown. "Do you wish to postpone these meetings?"

"That's hardly an option."

"I will make it an option if that is what you need."

"How can you be so nice to me right now?"

"How can I not?"

"It's my fault we're in this situation."

"Assigning blame is useless, but if you must do so, then assign me my portion. I was the one who waited too long to act on the intentions in the contract between our two families."

"I *knew* we weren't using birth control."

"Yes."

"Aren't you angry with me? You were furious yesterday."

"Yesterday is best left in the past."

And she knew he meant both literally the day before and their ill conceived night together.

"You're going to be a figure of public speculation and gossip for months because of this." And she knew how much that had to bother him.

"Highly doubtful. It will be a nine day's wonder. And I refuse to forget that had Elsa been more vindictive and less greedy, I would already be so."

The knowledge obviously weighed heavily on him. Angele could see it in the rigid tension of his shoulders and the haunted shadows in his gray eyes.

"That's in the past too."

He shrugged, but she knew he was too much of

a perfectionist to extend the same acceptance for mistakes to himself that he seemed determined to offer her.

"My own idiocy is not something I will forget anytime soon," he said, confirming her thoughts.

"So, we've both been idiots. It's time to move forward."

He laughed, the sound as surprising as it was surprised. "I do not believe anyone has called me an *idiot* in all my adult years."

"Not to your face anyway," she said, tongue in cheek.

His dark brows rose. "Not behind my back, either."

"Your arrogance is showing again."

"It is never very far below the surface, I assure you."

"What happened to the humble servant to your people?"

"The two are not mutually exclusive."

"Not in your world, anyway, right?"

"My world is your world."

"It is now."

"I could wish you were happier about that fact."

"It is what it is," she said, using the American vernacular for one of his favorite Arabic proverbs.

His jaw went taut, though nothing else gave away the fact her reply had not made him happy. "There was a time when you were nothing but pleased to be my intended."

"It's going to sound trite, but I grew up." She smiled, hoping to take any sting the words might have for him.

She wasn't trying to slight him, merely tell him the truth.

"Those words should be bitter, but from your mouth they are not."

Good. She was determined to live by her decision to accept her fate and stop whining, even internally. "I'm not bitter."

"Then there is great hope for our future."

"Yes, I suppose there is." They would never have the happy families fantasy she'd always dreamed of, but they could have a solid marriage and good life together.

She could do nothing but hope.

CHAPTER NINE

ANGELE'S HOPE FOR THE future seemed to prove true over the following weeks.

Often running interference with her family and his, Zahir willingly stayed in the States with Angele long enough for her to finalize preparations for her permanent move to Zohra. While she had to give up her apartment, he promised to buy a home with proper security for their trips back to U.S. in the future.

Announcement of their forthcoming wedding and the advent of their first child was met with a surprisingly positive response in both Zohra and Jawhar. The scandal rags didn't have much to report because the legitimate press had been given all the details along with photos of the "happy" couple together in both the United States and Zohra after she had officially relocated.

Zahir offered to handle the official press conference with his father, but Angele insisted on standing by his side. Begin as you mean to go on. That's what Lou-Belia had taught her and Angele had no intention of being a shrinking violet who spent her time hiding in the royal palace. They gave an interview to a leading personality reporter and Zahir made it very clear that he considered the "miscommunications" during their "courtship" to be his fault entirely.

His hero status was growing by the minute and not just with the public. Angele found herself falling more deeply in love with the man she was about marry than she'd ever been.

Crown Sheikh Zahir bin Faruq al Zohra was everything she had ever wanted in a husband and his behavior over the weeks leading to the wedding only reinforced that truth. He continued with what she privately termed his *unnecessary* courtship. After all, they were already headed for the altar with no chance at either of them backing out.

Nevertheless, he'd taken her to dinner both in Zohra's capital and such romantic hotspots like Paris—a high speed helicopter was an amazing form of transportation. Apparently it was good to be sheikh.

In addition to his attention, he showered her with gifts and more flowers, warning her he would be less than pleased to discover she'd been giving them away to the domestic staff as she had his first offerings.

She'd kept them all, pressing the loveliest for safekeeping. More the fool her.

It grew increasingly difficult to maintain her emotional distance, but she wasn't about to wear her heart on her sleeve like she had her whole life. Not when his was still so firmly encased behind a brick wall.

Angele saw no evidence that Zahir's feelings toward her had grown romantically. She didn't consider his courtship in that light. It was a politically expedient tactic that might be working, but wasn't fooling her where it counted.

In regard to his feelings.

In fact, with his absolute refusal to touch her with anything more than the briefest buss of his lips over hers in greeting or parting, she was fairly certain even the passion he'd briefly exhibited for her was long gone. While he'd shared her bed at the apartment, he always went to sleep long after her and was up before she opened her eyes in the morning.

Sure as certain, he never touched her intimately.

That didn't stop him from having more opinions regarding their wedding than even Lou-Belia could lay claim to. Angele didn't care what color of linens decorated the formal dining room, or how the royal crests of the Zohra and Jawhar were displayed.

Zahir cared about both and so much more. He'd even given Lou-Belia some advice concerning Angele's trousseau. Angele had no idea what that advice was, only that Lou-Belia was beside herself that he'd offered it.

"As if I do not know exactly what fashions would best suit my own daughter," her mother fumed as they traversed the high fashion district of Paris.

"I suppose it hasn't occurred to either of you that I've been choosing my own clothing for years now?" She'd been an editorial assistant on a fashion magazine, for heaven's sake.

Not that anyone seemed to remember that salient fact.

"You don't want my help shopping?" Lou-Belia asked, managing to sound both hurt and patently shocked.

"Of course, I want your company." Which was not the same thing, but she was hoping her mother would not notice.

Not that it mattered. By the end of the day, Angele had had her fill of both her mother and Zahir's advice. Not only had he taken her mother aside, but he'd called two of the couture shops they had appointments with and made recommendations for particular outfits for her try on.

His choices were rather sexy for a man who was back to treating her like a favored cousin.

When she muttered something to that effect, Lou-Belia said, "Nonsense. He's treating you with respect."

"I'd rather he treated me like a woman."

"Apparently he's already done that, or I wouldn't be looking forward to becoming a grandmother before the year is out."

Angele gave her mother a speaking glance, but shut up about Zahir's lack of interest in the physical side of their relationship.

She didn't stop thinking about it though. Every day he treated her like an ice princess instead of his princess brought back the pain of the years he'd ignored her for other pursuits. He'd promised her that he would not take a lover, but in the darkest hours of the night, Angele lay in her lonely bed and wondered.

Zahir helped Angele from the limousine, his bodyguards holding foreign reporters back. Their own people maintained a respectful distance, though their interest was just as avid.

It was not the first time he had brought his soon-to-be bride to one of the top restaurants in their capital for a romantic dinner. He was used to being stared at and talked about when he went into public. He was their future king. Naturally they would find him of interest.

And Angele handled the interest with aplomb, making him proud and not a little surprised by her perfected public persona.

Regardless, he usually preferred to keep his public profile to well-managed levels, but a ten-year-in-the-making courtship required extra efforts.

Not that they seemed to be making any impact on the woman who carried his child and would soon carry his name as well. She had retreated behind a smiling facade that irritated him beyond reason, because it was so different from the Angele he was accustomed to.

For as long as he could remember, Angele had

looked at him with a big dose of hero worship and not a small dose of want. He'd done his best to ignore the want because for too many years, she'd been all too young. Still, it had been there. And he had grown used to it. Had in fact, no idea how much he enjoyed that state of affairs until it was gone.

She was never anything less than pleasant, but she was also never anything more than pleasant. She might refute the title of princess because she could not claim it by birth and could not yet claim it by marriage, but she had the attitude down. Her aura of serenity could rival his mother's at dinner of State.

The problem was, that unlike his mother, Angele did not drop the serene little smiles and even tones when she was in the private company of family.

The vulnerable, sweet princess he had always known was now hidden behind the politically polished princess who had made her apologies to their people despite his willingness to take full responsibility for their *estrangement*.

Right now, although they were supposed to be spending time cementing their bond, her attention was firmly on those around them rather than him. Angele nodded and smiled to the Zohranians while managing to ignore the paparazzi yelling questions and taking their picture. And he had no reason to believe it would be any different once they were inside the restaurant, where she would no doubt maintain this infuriating distance.

Suddenly she dropped to her knees. He leaped forward, his body hovering over hers protectively while he looked around for some threat, even as he put his hand out to help her back to her feet. Which she ignored. It was only then that he realized a small child had managed to get away from his parents and through the small throng of reporters.

In her designer original gown, her face and hair perfectly coiffed, Angele opened her arms to the clearly frightened child. The little boy threw himself at what he obviously saw as safety.

She scooped him up, whispering something to the child that made him respond with a nod. All the while cameras flashed and Zahir had no problem imagining the front cover story of the social pages tomorrow.

Standing, Angele turned to him. "It appears we've made a friend."

Zahir smiled at the child giving him a shy sideways glance. "Hello, little man. Where are your parents?"

"Wanted to see the princess," the boy said instead of answering.

"I see. She is very special, is she not?"

The little boy nodded and Angele gave the child the first genuine smile he'd seen from her in days. "What is your name?"

Zahir didn't catch the muffled answer over a commotion going on to his right. The young girl his bodyguards allowed to come forward looking two parts terrified and one part awed, resembled the boy too much to be anything other than an older sister.

She confirmed Zahir's guess with her first words. "My brother didn't mean anything. I'm supposed to be watching him in the car while our parents run an errand, but we wanted to see the new princess."

"Please don't be upset." Angele gave another one of her genuine smiles to the girl. "He hasn't caused any trouble."

The girl did not look appreciably mollified. "My parents are going to be very angry."

"Perhaps they will not be so upset if they join us for dinner," Angele said.

The young girl stared as if she could not believe what Angele had said. The maître d', who had joined them outside, was looking at Angele with much the same expression on his usually unflappable face.

It was a politically brilliant move that would do much to shore up his princess' popularity with his people. And considering the lack of success of Zahir's attempts to romantically woo his bride-to-be, he didn't mind the extra company tonight.

Angele gave him a pleading look that had nothing in common with her new persona of serenity ice princess, and there was no chance he would kibosh the invitation. He turned to his bodyguard with instructions to find the parents and have them join the royal couple and their children in the restaurant for dinner.

He would have done far more for the genuine and warm gratitude now glowing in Angele's espresso-brown gaze.

Angele stood outside the secret passageway door to Zahir's rooms. Her hands were clammy and the nausea that had for the most part abated, was back in response to her jumping nerves.

This evening, she and Zahir had connected in a way they had not since she'd first seen the hurtful photos. She hoped they could connect in other ways tonight as well.

Before she could allow herself to change her mind, she lifted her hand and knocked on the panel. Then, without waiting for an answer, she pulled on the lever. It wasn't locked from the other side and the door swung inward.

A quick glance revealed that Zahir wasn't in the bedroom, so she crossed to the sitting room. His expression inquiring, he was standing up from a desk with an open laptop on its surface when she came in.

He'd discarded his robes of State and his suit jacket, as well as his tie. His shirt was unbuttoned at the neck, giving her a glimpse of the dark hair that covered his chest and the sleeves were rolled up to reveal his muscular forearms.

It was an intimate look, few would be privileged to see.

His eyes widened fractionally as they focused on her. "*Princess,* what are you doing here?"

"I wanted to thank you for allowing that family to have dinner with us." Angele had other plans as well, but she had enough diplomacy not to mention them right off the start.

"It was surprisingly enjoyable." He bent down and pressed a button on the laptop, sending it into hibernate.

So, he wasn't going to try to rush her out of there. Good. "Surprisingly?" she asked.

"I do not usually enjoy dining with strangers."

"You do it often enough in your official capacity."

"Exactly."

"Yet, you didn't hesitate to extend the invitation for them to join us when I asked." And that made her feel warm and gooey inside.

Was that pathetic? Did it matter? It was her life, after all. Not someone else's. She needed to live it for her happiness, or what she could grasp of it.

Which was why she was here, instead of chewing on all sorts of unpleasant possibilities for the future in her lonely bed.

He reached out and touched the corner of her

softly curved lips, an unreadable expression on his face. "I will always try to give you what you desire, when I can."

"I appreciate that." Did she need his love when she had his commitment?

She'd certainly felt cherished over the past weeks, even if his actions had not been driven by more tender feelings.

"We will be content together." He winced as if unhappy with his own choice of words.

"Contentment is not bad."

"No, there are far worse fates."

That there were better possible fates hung between them, unsaid, but not unappreciated. By them both, she felt. And she was not sure that meant what it once did.

Hope sparked a tiny light deep in her heart.

Taking her courage in her hands, she stepped firmly into his personal space. "You said you would always give me what I want."

"If it is within my power."

She nodded, pretty confident that what she

wanted was definitely within his power. Reaching out, she laid her hands on his biceps and then curled her fingers around the hard muscles there. She smoothed her thumbs along his arms and he made no move to stop her. The knowledge she was allowed to do this shuddered through her.

He was hers, as she was his.

One day this man would be King of all Zohra, but from the day she had agreed to marry him, he had been *her man*. And always would be. All man, all hers. Even if his birthright made him larger than life in every other way.

"Angele?" he asked in a strangled voice.

He wanted her. And it wasn't just his voice that gave him away. All sorts of little indicators showed she affected him powerfully, if she was looking for them. And she was looking. His nostrils flared, his pupils were dilated and the muscles beneath her fingers were rigid with tension.

The passion was not gone, merely banked. Relief strengthened her resolve. "You want me."

"Yes."

"Make love to me."

"I cannot."

She let her gaze drift down the front of him. His tailored suit trousers did nothing to hide the rigid length behind his placket.

She smiled, her nerves settling just a bit. "I think, in fact, that you can."

He laughed, the sound warm and filled with real humor. "Physically I am more than able. I am aching, *Aziz*."

Her breath caught. Did he realize he'd called her beloved? But then, men in this part of the world often called their wives such. It did not mean that he loved her.

Still, it did mean he saw her as his to treasure.

"Then, let me assuage that ache."

"I would like nothing more."

"What is stopping you?"

"I gave my word to your father that I would not take advantage of you prior to our official wedding."

She latched onto the word *official*. She'd suspected something since that night, now she would confirm it. "You already consider me your wife."

He said nothing.

She challenged him with her gaze. "Tell the truth."

"I do," he gritted out. "You are my wife."

It was romantic really, though she wasn't about to admit it. "Possessive."

"Yes."

"I came to you in a wedding gown and you made me promises you never spoke out loud," she guessed. "It was the only way you would accept the gift of my virginity."

"Yes."

She smiled.

He growled. "I am an old-fashioned man, but I am not naff."

Angele suppressed the desire to giggle. He sounded so put-upon. "No, I'd never accuse you of being sappy." But she couldn't deny the old-fashioned label.

Even Elsa had been an example of that. Zahir had been a man in his sexual prime when he signed the agreement for their eventual marriage. He needed a sexual outlet and he'd looked for one.

Angele had no doubt he hadn't expected to feel anything real for Elsa, or for the affair to last as long as it did. Knowing he had cared so much, that Elsa had been able to hurt him, hurt Angele. However, it was over and he was truly hers now, in every way.

"Does the future king of Zahir allow another man to determine the parameters of his life?" she challenged.

"I made a promise."

"Not to take advantage, but how is it taking advantage when in your heart, I'm already your wife?"

"And in your heart?" it was his turn to challenge.

She could give him nothing less than the truth. "I'm yours, Zahir. I always have been."

"That's not what you said in your letter, or that press release."

"I wanted to give you your freedom."

"So I could find *true love*."

She was sure he meant to say the words true love with more sarcasm, but his tone carried more confusion than cynicism.

And suddenly, she realized something very important. Just because he was not in love with her did not mean Zahir did not need her love. In fact, she was no longer fully convinced he did not love her, either. After some fashion anyway. There was something there, something she did not yet understand, but she was determined to.

"You hold yourself back from me," she said, not as an accusation but as bait.

She needed to understand this complicated man. Angele would be the first to admit, she'd been so blinded by her own emotions, she had all but ignored his.

One thing had remained true for ten years, though. This man had always intended to marry her and by his own admission, he had intended to bring his formidable honor to bear in remaining faithful to her.

"I would say you are the one that has put up walls between us." He frowned, though he did not move away from her.

If she didn't know better, she would think he was no more capable of doing so than she was.

"You think?" she asked, wanting…maybe even needing to hear this from his mouth.

"You used to love me."

"I still do." And denying it to both of them was doing nothing but hurting the man she had no desire to hurt and herself.

She hadn't shocked him with her request they make love, but her words of love made him jerk back as if struck. "No, you do not."

She moved closer again, so their bodies were less than a breath apart. "I do."

"You do not smile at me as you used to."

"The last few weeks have been stressful." And she'd thought they would be better off if she buried her deeper emotions, so they came to each other on a level playing field. But hiding her feelings was not natural to her, not like it was for him.

In order to do so, she'd had to cut off her emotions completely, hiding behind what she called her political female figure facade. She'd had plenty of examples growing up, but it was only tonight she'd realized how much the constant facade had been smothering her.

She needed to be herself sometimes, but most particularly with him.

"Love is not required in a marriage such as ours is to be, but both parties should like each other, I think." He sounded like he was trying to convince himself as much as her.

Instead of allowing herself to get upset at this further evidence he didn't love her, she listened to what he *wasn't* saying. She heard his need, a need she doubted he allowed anyone else to glimpse.

"I do like you, Zahir, and I love you." It was

easier to admit now that she'd already said it. "I never stopped."

He reversed their hold so that it was his hands holding her close, with no hope of moving away. "You are mine. I will never let you leave me again."

"I'm not going anywhere." She needed him and was coming to accept that on some very important level he needed her, too. "I want you to make love to me."

"And my promise to your father?"

"Is nullified if making love is an act of caring rather than slaking mere physical desire."

"Of course I care for you. You have always been as important to me as any of my family. That has not changed."

It wasn't the romantic declaration of the century, but for Zahir those words were a promise of commitment deeper than most men were even capable of making.

"I believe you."

Then, it was if something inside him broke.

Maybe it was his self-control, because he took her mouth like an invading army intent on total conquest.

CHAPTER TEN

SENSING he needed this as much as she did, she allowed her body to melt into him in a surrender powered by her own desire. And was that really surrender at all, or a victory?

She certainly felt like she was winning as his lips drew forth passion that even surpassed the single night they had shared together.

He swung her up in his arms and headed toward the bedroom, though his mouth never left hers. Part of her marveled that they didn't bump into walls or doorjambs, but then this was Zahir. The man could navigate the minefield of world politics, his own rooms were no challenge.

They came down onto the bed together, his heavy body covering hers, proof of his desire pressed into her stomach. Taking the kiss to the next level, he thrust against her, his essence surrounding and grounding her, blocking out everything else.

Heated moisture soaked the scrap of fabric between her legs and she spread them, seeking more stimulation. But there were too many layers in the way, her own outfit preventing her from getting as close to him as she wanted to. She whimpered, wanting it and every other bit of clothing off her.

He made a sound of satisfaction as he continued to kiss her with a masterful passion that was far beyond what he had shown her before. It was as if that night he'd been treating her like she'd been made of spun-glass. And perhaps since it had been her first time, he'd been right to do so.

But now, there was an elemental, almost primal power radiating through every kiss, every caress.

And his hands were everywhere, clever fingers that knew how to draw forth urges and sensations she hadn't even known she was capable of. Her clothes came off and so did his, though she couldn't remember the sequence or even who took off what.

But the moment when he pressed her hands upward and curled her fingers around the wrought-iron spindles on the big bed's headboard and told her not to let go was seared into her mind like his passion seared her heart.

She stared at him. "Why?"

"I want to pleasure you."

"And I need to keep my hands here for you to do that?"

"It will please me."

She didn't understand. She wanted to touch him, but she wanted to do what he asked, too. The idea of giving total control over to him both alarming and very, very alluring.

"You're kinky!" she accused with equal parts shock and desire.

"I am a man who knows what he desires." That was so not a denial.

"You like being in control."

"This surprises you?"

"No." Though maybe it should. Wouldn't a man who had to control so much, want to give a little up?

His fierce, primal expression said, *not this one.* Not her sheikh.

He arranged her legs so that they were bent at the knee and spread apart in a wanton display that would have embarrassed her if she wasn't so excited.

"Will it always be like this?" she asked breathlessly. Would he always want this extra bit of control?

He looked up from his heated perusal of her most intimate flesh. "I do not know. I have never done this before, but it is something I have long wanted."

She moaned, the words more effective than any touch. "I'm glad this is special between us."

"Everything we share in our marriage bed is special. No woman has ever belonged to me as you do and I have never belonged to another woman as I do to you."

"What do you mean?" He was far from a virgin.

"You own my future." With that he touched her sweet spot, his fingers going on to thoroughly explore every bit of intimate flesh exposed so fully to his gaze. "You are so beautiful."

"I don't think women are beautiful there."

"You know this because you have looked?" he asked teasingly.

Even knowing he was teasing, she still jerked in shock. "Zahir! Of course not!" She'd never seen female *parts* outside of a sex education book and those were clinical diagrams.

"Then you cannot know, so I will forgive your doubt."

She turned her face away, embarrassed and pleased and even more embarrassed because she was pleased.

"Every inch of you is beautiful, including this flesh only I and your doctor will ever see."

That had her looking at him again. "You didn't used to think I was beautiful."

"You were thirteen when our contract was signed. To have looked upon you in that light would have been wrong."

"I didn't stay thirteen."

"In my mind, you did."

She almost laughed, but the seriousness in his expression could not be denied. A jolt of unexpected understanding went through her. Perhaps this, more than anything else, explained the passage of ten years since that darned contract had been signed.

She stopped wondering seconds later when his touch robbed every logical, and illogical for that matter, thought from her brain. He knew exactly how to touch her, playing with her breasts and teasing her nipples into turgid aching nubs.

But he didn't stop there; no, he seemed to know secrets about her body that had escaped her notice. Caressing her inner thigh, that spot in the center of her back, her nape, he stimulated numerous little bundles of nerve endings she'd had no idea existed on her body. Even after that first night together.

She writhed, begging him to come inside her and finish this spiral of pleasure, but she did not let go of the headboard.

He rewarded her with his mouth. First on her breasts, then the other hot spots he'd exposed on her body and then finally on that place he said was beautiful to him.

She was still screaming out her first orgasm when he surged inside, filling her beyond comprehension.

Just as the first time, it wasn't merely her body he filled, but her heart and her mind until she could not breathe without breathing him in, could not think without thinking of him, could not feel without feeling him.

Her second orgasm came over in a wave of such intense pleasure, it bordered on pain.

He wasn't done yet, though. He held himself rigid through her body's convulsions and only started moving again when her breathing had slowed down to hiccupping pants.

He brushed at the tears she hadn't even realized she'd been crying. *"Aziz."*

"I love you, Zahir."

Something moved in his gaze and then he started to move again, this time building to a rhythm that left her gasping with no sound for her scream when she reached the pinnacle of pleasure again…with him.

He insisted she sleep in his bed that night after they bathed together; she rested better than she had since returning from the States, her body, mind and heart as at peace as they could be.

She woke the next morning to gentle hands moving over her body. She went to reach for him, but her hands were stuck and it was then she realized they were bound to the headboard with something made of the softest silk.

"Zahir?" she asked as her eyes opened to the shadows of early dawn.

His look was as intent as she'd ever seen it. "Is it all right?"

Perhaps another woman would say no. Perhaps with another man, she should. But Angele knew what Zahir was asking her and it wasn't just whether or not she was willing to let him make love to her with her hands bound.

He was asking if she trusted him enough to allow it.

The only things she knew about kink were the jokes passed around the water cooler at her former job, but this was instinctive. She didn't need to know about anyone else's intimacy to know this was right between her and Zahir.

He needed to know she trusted him completely and if she was honest with herself, and she always tried to be, she needed to know the same thing. This binding was for both their sakes, a chance to undo the damage too many years between the signing of the contract and their actual wedding had wrought.

It wasn't a declaration of love, but it was one of intent.

She could accept it. "Yes. It's all right."

The tension in the lines around his eyes dissipated and he smiled, happiness glowing forth in a way she'd never seen from him. "You are so alluring this way."

And he was unbearably sexy with that look of joy in his eyes. He might not love her, but then again he might. No matter what had been said on the subject to this point. One thing was certain, though: she was able to give him something no one else could. He'd told her he'd never tried this type of thing with another woman and she believed him.

He would not trust a casual lover not to go to the tabloids with the sexual peccadilloes of the Crown Sheikh of Zohra.

He was a man who must maintain personal control at all times and had far too much responsibility on his plate for any normal man. But he was not an average guy, not even close.

He was something more and so was this. Something special and incredible.

"Will you ever let me turn the tables?" she asked, not sure she wanted to, but curious.

"If you'd like." And she knew he meant it. He was willing to trust her in ways he would *never* have trusted another.

"Maybe someday…" she said, the last word trailing off into a moan as his heated mouth made love to her body.

Rich male humor sounded even as he upped the stakes and drove her toward pleasure only he had ever been able to give her.

Zahir accompanied Angele on the walk back to her room, shrugging when she commented that if they were caught together in the secret passageway there could be no doubt what they had been up to. "You are mine."

"You're a possessive man."

"And are you any less possessive?"

She didn't even have to think about it. "No."

"Good."

"I thought men didn't like clingy women?"

He stopped them in the passageway outside her room and gave her a serious look that melted her right to her toes. "Cling, *Princess*."

She choked out a disbelieving laugh as his mouth covered hers in a kiss of unmistakable claiming.

When their mouths separated, he sighed. "I have business of State in Europe. My flight leaves later this morning and I will be in meetings until then."

"Where in Europe?"

"Germany."

Her breath caught, but she wasn't giving in to jealousy. He'd told her to cling. Had he meant it? "Berlin's Fashion Week is happening right now. I could come with you and write a freelance article. I'm sure I could get into some of the runway shows."

"If you are sure you can get away from the wedding preparations." His smile was brilliant.

His reaction left no doubt he wanted Angele to come. This was no grudging acceptance. She'd never be a whiny-clingy type, but she knew that wasn't what he meant. Zahir wanted to know that no matter how independent she was by nature, that she needed him and would make time to be with him.

"Lou-Belia and your mother have it under control."

"You have given them full control of the festivities."

She wasn't sure if that was an observation or a criticism, but she chose to take it as the former. "You may as well realize that planning social events is not my thing. I've got a great attention to detail and can coordinate my life to the Nth degree, but I don't enjoy poring over guest lists and seating charts."

He nodded, as if confirming his own thoughts. "It is not a requirement of your position. We have a more than competent event coordination team."

"I know. The palace event coordinator is pulling his hair out at both our mothers' overt interference in every detail of the wedding."

"My mother said you will not allow any one to see the dress you have planned to wear for the formal ceremony?"

"That's one thing I refuse to compromise on."

"Mother said you won't tell them anymore than that it is white."

Was he fishing? And was it for his sake, or his mother's? Angele knew both Lou-Belia and Queen Adara were frustrated by Angele's secrecy on the matter.

She wasn't giving in, though. "That's all they need to know."

"She said you told her that it would not clash with the traditional couture chosen for the rest of the family and wedding party."

Angele merely shrugged. If he thought she was giving him any more details than she'd given his mother, he was wrong. No matter how sexy she found him and his interest in their wedding.

Though if he knew her as well as she had

come to realize he probably did, he would realize exactly what she planned to wear to speak her vows.

Angele napped on the flight to Germany. The night before hadn't seen either of them sleeping much, though Zahir didn't seem affected in the least as he worked in his seat beside her on the private royal jet.

Her morning hadn't been exactly relaxing, either. Lou-Belia had come close to meltdown when Angele told her she was flying to Germany with Zahir. Angele had spent the remaining hours on wedding preparations, despite the fact someone else could easily have made the calls and decisions she ostensibly made. Ostensibly because all she did was rubber stamp approval plans already put in place by her mother or Queen Adara.

Angele had exactly twenty minutes to pack for the trip. It was a good thing she was used to travel.

They were in the limousine, driving away from the airport, before she realized there was a real possibility Zahir would take her to the chalet in the photos that had prompted her to try to break their contract. She didn't like that possibility. Not one little bit.

"Where are we staying?"

He named a posh hotel in downtown Berlin.

Stifling any sign of the abject relief she felt, she couldn't help probing. "I thought you owned a chalet you used when doing business here."

"It's been sold as have most of our business interests here in Germany." He looked at her as if challenging her to ask further.

She wasn't sure she wanted to. "Oh."

Either she trusted him, or she didn't. She chose to.

"We couldn't cut all ties—it wasn't what was best for Zohra, but they have been minimized," he added in the silence that followed.

She felt she should respond to that in some

way, but wasn't sure how. She finally settled on a quiet, "Thank you."

"No thanks needed." His words were more forceful, as if trying to impart a message he did not want to come right out and say.

And apparently, that was that, because he didn't say anything further and answered his phone when it buzzed in his pocket. However, she felt a lightness in her heart that could not be denied.

Their connecting hotel suites were both luxurious and comfortable. His comment that she could use the bedroom in hers as a dressing room put paid to any doubt she might have about where she would be sleeping over the next three days.

Despite the fact that she now traveled with a security entourage, Angele found no difficulty in getting last minute VIP seating for the main runway shows. It was past midnight when she made it back to the hotel that night. She was tired, but wired.

"You really love the world of fashion, don't you?" Zahir asked.

She shrugged as she kicked off her pumps. "What can I say? It's in my genes."

"Fashion is a lucrative industry."

"It is."

"Considering how little you like to plan events, I do not suppose you would consider coordinating a fashion week in our capital?"

Excitement made her heart rate increase. A fashion week, or even a single runway show was nowhere near as boring an event as a State dinner. "That depends. Can I hire a team to help me? Can we designate a charity to couple with and make the event about more than just fashion?"

"Of course."

"Then, yes, absolutely. I would love to."

"Good."

"It's no longer seen as quite the thing for a political wife to be without some interests of her own," she acknowledged.

The British weren't the only country that pushed a princess to be more than her title.

"Just so."

She smiled, enjoying the fact he had thought about what sort of interest would make her happy. Because she knew Zahir was not a spontaneous guy. "You've been thinking about this for a while."

"Years."

Wow. Just, wow. "I thought so. I could have continued writing freelance fashion articles, you know. We don't have to invent an industry for me."

"I'm sure you will continue the writing. You are very good, but it is time Zohra joined the rest of the world in showcasing modern fashion."

"Right, like you really care if there is a runway show in Zohra's capital."

"What is important to you, is important to me."

She threw her arms around him and hugged him. "I just love you so much, right now."

He laughed, his eyes going hot with an expression she was coming to know very well. "That is good to hear."

She cocked her head to the side and smiled up at him. "I don't want our children raised by nannies."

"Agreed."

So, a very part-time interest. She could work with that.

"Are you ready for bed?" he asked.

"I'm tired, but not sleepy."

"I think I can fix that."

And he did.

CHAPTER ELEVEN

THE next day, she got up early and when he left for his meetings, she accompanied him. The car dropped her and her security detail off at the main pavilion. She spent her morning focused on the German designers and boutiques, taking dozens of pictures in between miniinterviews with designers, boutique owners and other attendees of the show. It was unsurprising, but nevertheless pleasing how eager people were to be quoted in an article written by the soon-to-be wife of the Crown Sheikh of Zohra.

Her pregnancy caught up with her around lunchtime and she returned to the hotel for a nap after eating a light snack from the food stalls.

She woke up hungry and decided on a late lunch in the hotel restaurant before returning to the Fashion Week festivities.

The *hauptkellner* looked surprised to see her, but then nodded to himself as if working something out. He said something in rapid German to another waiter that she was sure Zahir would understand, but Angele's German was not up to such rapid speech. Then he turned and led her toward the back of the restaurant, where the tables afforded a lovely view of the garden out the wall of windows.

She was so intent on the view she didn't immediately see the other occupants at the table the head waiter had stopped beside. He snapped his fingers and the other waiter appeared with a third chair, since the two already at the table were occupied.

By Zahir.

And Elsa Bosch.

Zahir's face had gone completely blank, but Elsa looked both amused and slightly sick to her stomach.

It was an interesting reaction that Angele cataloged almost subconsciously as she took the chair the waiter held out for her. The *hauptkellner* placed her napkin in her lap while the waiter laid another place setting at the table.

He went to hand her a menu, but she waved it away. "I'll just have a chicken Caesar salad."

She didn't know if they had it on the menu, but was confident the chef could come up with something. It was taking all her concentration to maintain an air of calm and casual demeanor while seated at the table with her soon-to-be husband and his former mistress.

The waiters left and Angele released a breath she hadn't realized she'd been holding. "Well, this is awkward."

Neither of her companions had an answer for that, so she turned to Zahir. "Not to be rude, but I believe you told me this particular problem had been taken care of."

Elsa made a sound of annoyance, but didn't say anything.

"I believed it had, but then further developments arose."

"She's trying to blackmail you now?" Angele asked in Arabic, fairly confident none of their fellow diners could overhear to quote her for the gossip rags.

She made no attempt to hide either her disgust or her shock. Only an idiot risked making an absolute enemy of a man like Zahir.

"No."

"I am not sure if that makes me more relieved or worried." Perhaps a week ago, her reaction to this situation would have been much different. Okay, there was no maybe about it, but she'd decided to trust him. Totally and completely.

And she was going to keep doing so, unless she was given a whole lot more than a public lunch as evidence she shouldn't.

"Elsa was not the blackmailer."

Angele's gaze flicked to the other woman, who seemed to be listening with interest. "No? You confirmed she was."

"She did not deny it when I confronted her and threatened to bankrupt and dismantle her personal production company if so much as a single picture from that envelope ever found its way into the press."

"I imagine a tell-all article would have paid her well enough to tempt her regardless."

"I was more than generous in our parting. She signed a contract stipulating absolute media silence in exchange and would have to pay back every penny I ever gave her or spent on her if she broke it."

"So, how could she think she would get away with blackmail?"

"She didn't."

"It was my brother," Elsa spoke in English, but made it clear she had enough understanding of Arabic to have followed the gist of their conversation.

"Your brother?" Angele asked in the same language, feeling shock on shock.

"He hadn't signed anything." Elsa shrugged. "He's an idiot. He did not realize that the way the contract was worded that I had signed, it wouldn't matter. I would still have to pay the price."

"Elsa is here to pass over all the printed copies of the pictures as well as her brother's hard drive and backup thumb drive."

"He could still have other copies."

"He doesn't," Elsa said.

"I'm supposed to take your word for it?" Angele asked, maintaining a tone of slightly bored interest for which she was rather proud, considering the maelstrom of emotions roiling inside her.

Elsa's shoulders gave an elegant roll, sort of a shrug and sort of something else.

Angele's gaze flicked to Zahir to see his reaction, but his eyes were fixed intently on her and her alone.

"Do you believe her?" Angele asked him.

"It does not matter if I do, or not."

"Because you will not leave it to chance."

"No. Even as we speak, he is on his way to Zohra to face blackmail charges."

"What?" Elsa demanded a lot louder than was probably wise.

Zahir finally settled his gaze on her and Angele shivered. She wouldn't want that look fixed on her. Ever.

"I am not convinced you were unaware of your brother's schemes. In fact, I can almost guarantee he's too stupid to have considered Angele the better target."

Elsa blanched.

"If he names you as accomplice, expect extradition proceedings."

"But you can't do this. I brought you the pictures."

"Thank you. They and your brother's hard drive will be used as evidence in his trial."

Elsa looked stunned. "But that's not fair."

Angele wondered at the other woman's lack of understanding of the way that Zahir thought and the type of action that thought process would lead to.

"And you think blackmail is fair?" he asked,

not sounding like he really cared if she did, or not.

"But you said you would not prosecute if I ceased and desisted."

Had Zahir ever really fallen for that damsel in distress act? Angele could barely suppress the need to roll her eyes.

Looking as unimpressed as she could hope, Zahir said, "That was when I believed you to be the culprit. I owed you some level of protection, regardless of how things ended between us."

He *was* an old-fashioned guy. He'd said so on more than one occasion. Zahir would not have sent Elsa to prison, unless she forced him to it. Her brother, on the other hand, was another matter. Being a man, being someone willing to trade on his sister's former relationship, in Zahir's eyes, Mr. Bosch was fair game.

"But Hans wasn't going to do anything more."

"Really?"

"Of course."

Zahir looked intently at the other woman, as if

weighing her veracity. Angele, for one, believed her or at least that Elsa believed what she'd said.

"Then, explain the blackmail letter Angele's father received last week."

"My father?" Angele asked in shock as Elsa's perfectly painted mouth opened and closed like a landed carp.

Zahir returned his gaze to Angele. "Yes. Cemal came to me immediately with the demand."

"Oh, stop harping." Elsa frowned at him. "You make Hans sound like a criminal when he was just trying his luck."

"I did not say it was Hans, *Aziz*."

Elsa gasped and then glared at them both. "So, that's it. You've tricked me into naming my brother and providing you with evidence against him."

"Would you prefer to face the charges on your own?" Zahir asked pitilessly.

Once again, the other woman went pale, this time her hands shaking as she went for a sip of her white wine. "No."

"I thought not."

"I could still go to the tabloids with my story."

"You've tied all your money up in your productions company. You can't afford to pay me back."

"So sue me for the money, the story will be out there for all the world to see."

"I have already released an official statement admitting a past liaison with you that I deeply regret along with the news that your brother will be tried for blackmail in my country." He was speaking to Elsa, but looking at Angele, as if her reaction was the only one that mattered.

"That sounds like the smartest move you could make." He'd shown her with news of the baby that in some cases transparency circumvented a media frenzy.

Once again Elsa did her carp impression and this time it was even less attractive than the last. "I…"

Zahir turned back to her. "Would do well to keep your media silence. Or you will pay the price for your poor judgment just as your brother must pay the price for his."

"But that's all it was, it was poor judgment. He can't go to prison for that."

"Poor judgment that leads to breaking the law also leads to jail." Zahir shrugged and stood. "It is the way of things."

He put his hand out to Angele. "Come, *ya habibti*."

She stood without hesitation. She still had plenty of questions for Zahir, but they could wait for privacy. She turned to Elsa before leaving. "You have a choice right now."

Elsa said nothing, but cocked her head as if inviting Angele to continue.

"Zahir forgave your betrayal and was willing to overlook even worse in his eyes because of your shared past. Don't make him an enemy now."

"Isn't he already?"

"If he was, you would be on the plane with Hans right now."

"He's my brother."

"I understand that, but he broke the law and my guess is this isn't the first time."

Elsa's flinch confirmed Angele's supposition.

"It's just the first time he's had to pay for it. Believe it, or not, Zahir is doing Hans a favor."

"How do you work that out?"

"The next time, your brother could have attempted to blackmail the wrong person. That person might not take legal recourse, but something far more permanent than a few years in prison."

"But prison in Zohra."

"*Isn't* a third-world hellhole. It's prison. With family visitation and guards who face far stricter reprisal for corruption than most other developed nations."

Elsa's eyes filled with tears, but she nodded. "I'm not stupid. I'm not going to the media with a tell-all."

"I appreciate it."

"He was always yours."

"I've come to realize that."

"I deserved a chance at happiness." Elsa meant the man she'd betrayed Zahir with.

"Yes, you did. But so do we."

"Can he serve his time in a German prison?" Elsa asked Zahir without looking at him. "At least then, I could visit him often."

Zahir did not answer, but Angele gave the other woman a look meant to convey her intention of discussing the matter with him. Elsa must have gotten it because she nodded slightly.

The waiter was coming with Angele's salad as she and Zahir walked away from the table. Zahir instructed the clearly confused man to have her food delivered to his suite.

Neither Zahir nor Angele spoke on the elevator ride up to their floor. Once they were in his room, he let out a deep sigh, but didn't say anything, either.

"Was this the State business you had to take care of?"

"No, but the other business made a good cover for handling this issue." Zahir looked like he was waiting for something.

An explosion perhaps? Only Angele didn't feel like exploding.

"Do you have any more work you have to do today?" she asked him.

"No."

"Would you like to come to the Fashion Week with me?"

She didn't think she'd ever seen Zahir looking so nonplussed.

And then he frowned. "No. And I would prefer you did not leave, either."

"Why is that?"

"You know why."

"Spell it out for me."

"We need to talk."

"About?"

"About what happened in the dining room, damn it." Zahir rarely cursed in her presence.

She took heart in it. He was upset. And while

maybe she should feel badly about that, she was actually pleased. "What exactly did you want to talk about?"

"You caught me having a meal with my former mistress."

"You were gathering evidence for the court case against her brother."

"You would expect me to have told you my plans prior to meeting him. I'm sure you are further angered by the fact I did not tell you about the attempt to blackmail your father."

"Nope." She thought about it to make sure and then shook her head. "Not angry."

He opened his mouth, but then closed it again without speaking.

"You wanted to protect me from upset while I was pregnant."

"I cannot guarantee I would behave differently if you were not pregnant," he said, as if admitting some deep dark secret.

"I get that."

"You do?"

"What do you think I mean when I tell you that I love you, Zahir?"

"I do not know."

"That's becoming more than a little apparent. I don't just love the bits about you I find comfortable. I know you see the world through eyes influenced by generations of responsibility that comes with your role. You protect your family, you protect your people, you protect me. It's in your DNA."

"That does not bother you?"

"I'm not promising never to get angry, or call you out over it, but for the most part? It makes me feel safe. Cherished."

"I do cherish you."

"I believe you."

"You do?" his voice was tinged with wonder.

She smiled. Nodded. "I do."

"I did not want you under more stress than you already are."

"I understand."

"You do?"

"Yes. I would do the same for you."

For once, it was easy to read her world leader love's facial expression. Utter shock and a shade of disbelief.

She laughed. "Don't you think your mother has ever protected your father from stress when she could?"

"Yes, but…"

"No buts, we'll both protect each other."

"Do you think I am being too harsh on Elsa's brother?"

"No, but if you can work it out so he serves his time closer to his sister, I think that would be good."

Zahir nodded. "It will be done."

"For me, but not for her?" she asked, curious that he had shown no indication of even hearing the other woman's request.

"Yes."

"She said you've always been mine."

"You said you believed her."

"I do. I didn't for a while," Angele admitted. "I do now, though."

"What changed?"

"I figured out that you love me."

"What?"

"I'm not even sure you haven't always loved me, but you wouldn't let yourself consider such a thing because I stayed thirteen in your mind. You transferred your feelings for me onto Elsa, but not enough to allow you to even consider marrying her instead of me."

"How...I..." He went silent for several long moments, took a deep breath and let it out. "You're right."

"Say it."

"I will on our wedding day."

"Yes, you will, but you'll say it now, too."

"Now who is being bossy?"

"You'd be bored silly with a pushover."

"I love you."

She started to cry, but he didn't say anything. How could he? His own eyes were just as wet.

He made her eat the salad before taking her into the bedroom and laying her gently on the bed.

"Another wedding night?" she asked softly as he divested them both of their clothes.

"A night of affirmation. I love you beyond reason. It is not an emotion I ever thought to experience. I know now what I felt in the past was lust mixed with relief at being just a man, for a few short hours. But I realized something, I've never been able to leave my role behind… not even when I was with her. Only with you, can I be what I am and still be free to be just a man."

"You are the man I love, the man I have always loved." Her words came out breathless as he touched her in places that made her quiver, squirm and moan.

"And you are the woman I love, will always love." And then he proved it with his body, making gentle, long love to her, repeating the words in every language he spoke fluently and a few he did not.

When he yelled out *Aziz* when he climaxed, she knew she really was his beloved.

EPILOGUE

ANGELE wore the dress Zahir had given her on their first night together for their wedding, making his mother cry and his father beam with unadulterated joy. Their wedding celebration lasted a full week before he took her on a honeymoon to Paris, telling her it was appropriate for them.

It was the City of Lovers after all.

They were at the top of the Eiffel Tower when he wrapped his arms around her, pulling her into his body as they looked out over the City of Light. "Beautiful."

"It is." She snuggled back against him. "I want to hold this moment in my heart forever."

"We can get my bodyguard to take a picture."

She smiled. He was a crown sheikh; they went nowhere without security, but sometimes that came in handy. Like when getting snapshots of their honeymoon highlights.

At least the security detail didn't share their suite, just had rooms on either side of them.

"Let's," she said, in answer to his suggestion.

He made the request in Arabic and then bent down to kiss her as their guard pressed the button for their picture with Paris at night in the background.

She was breathless and bemused when Zahir lifted his head.

"You are in all the pictures of my future that my heart can see."

She accepted his words for truth. She understood…she'd never seen a future for herself without him in it, no matter how hard she'd tried to for that brief time.

No wonder he refused to dismiss the idea of an arranged marriage for their child.

It had certainly worked out for them.

* * * * *